RUN LITTLE WOLF

The Forest Pack Series

G. BAILEY

THE FOREST PACK SERIES BY G.
BAILEY

INTERNATIONAL BESTSELLING AUTHOR

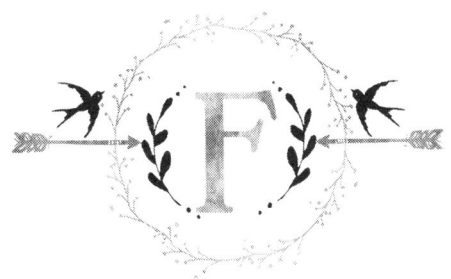

Cover Design by Olivia Pro Design

I'm English, so please ignore the strange words.

Ever heard the saying, never follow the big bad wolf into the woods?
Well, I wish I had listened to Little Red Riding Hoods advice.

One bite. That's all it took to turn Harper into a wolf and change her entire life. Turning eighteen was meant to be a fun night out, a party in the woods to celebrate with friends, but it ends in disaster. Harper wakes up in a car, on her way to a pack of wolves; ones she must live with. The sexy and alluring alpha welcomes her, declaring her his mate. Only Harper's best friend, a vampire she grew up with, tells her she belongs with him. Now, Harper must keep her mates from destroying each other.To make matters worse, the wolves are at war with other kinds of shifters. When one of them turns up, demanding she is their mate, will her alpha, who she rejected, fight for her?
Will the vampire, who loves her, help her pack?

For Rosalie, whose favourite fairy tale inspired this book.

CHAPTER ONE

HARPER

"Really? A party in the woods? *That's* where you want to spend your eighteenth birthday?" Colton asks me, just as the school bell rings, signalling the end of class *and* the last day of school for us. It's finally over, and to celebrate, everyone is going to this party in the woods tonight. Well, everyone except Colton, that is, and he hasn't stopped asking me why I want to go, since I told him this morning of my plans. I chuck my books in my bag, looking around at all my classmates as they run out the door, all of them so happy to leave.

"Yes, why won't you come?" I ask, pulling my

coat on and picking up my bag. He grins at me - a cheeky grin that matches his personality. Colton is every bit the typical hot guy in looks, with short blond hair, bright blue eyes, and golden skin. In fact, when he spoke to me for the first time, last year, I choked on my drink and blurted out a load of words that made no sense. While I was utterly mortified with myself, he still wanted to be my friend. He's a strange guy, but we quickly became best friends.

"I just can't, not at night," he mutters, pushing a hand through his hair. It's a nervous tick of his.

"You know, I never see you out at night. Are your parents really that strict?" I ask. He always leaves my house before the sun sets and he never wants to go out after school in the winter because it gets dark so quick. I met his parents once, and they didn't like me; at least, I don't think they did, considering they never replied to me when I said hello, and only asked Colton what he was doing by bringing me home with him.

"Something like that." He smiles, but it almost seems a little sad. "Let's go and get some lunch. I have a gift for you," Colton says, and holds his hand out for me. I take it as we leave the classroom.

"Why do you always hold my hand, Colt?" I ask

him, and he smiles down at me as we stroll through the nearly empty corridors.

"I want to, it's that simple," he says, and shrugs his shoulders.

"You should hold hands with a girlfriend, not me. This is why you don't have one." I lift our joined hands and he laughs.

"I don't have one because I don't want one, Harper." He nudges my shoulder. "Plus, every girl here is too scared of you to try and hit on me."

"What eighteen-year-old guy doesn't want a girlfriend? And I'm not that bad," I laugh.

"This one. And yes, you are. You glare at them when they speak to me," he says. To be fair, I don't exactly glare. It's just, the Barbie dolls that try to hit on Colton aren't good enough for him. Colton needs a sweet girlfriend, someone kind and not made of mostly plastic. I roll my eyes and stop as Skye runs up to us in the car park. Skye is my only other friend in this school, in this village. Growing up in foster care isn't easy; bouncing from house to house isn't any better. When I moved here last year, no one would talk to me until I met Skye. And then I met Colton.

"Harper, are you still coming tonight?" she asks, stopping in front of me, not even looking at me as she talks. No, her eyes are on Colton. Not that he even looks her way; he never has. Skye has tried to get me to set her up with him on several different occasions, but I don't know how many times I've told her that he isn't interested. I *do* get her interest, even I have to admit Colton is extremely good-looking compared to the guys at this school. Or any school I've ever been to, for that matter.

"Yeah, I will meet you there at eight." I smile at her, even though I'm getting annoyed at how she acts around Colton. I roll my eyes as she twirls her blonde hair around her finger and steps closer to him.

"Are you coming, Colt? I know I would love to see you there," she says, her words laced with suggestion. She may as well strip down naked and lay herself out for him at this rate.

"No, it's Harper's birthday and I have plans for her. See you around, Skye," he says, tugging on my hand as she frowns. I give her a small smile as I walk past her with Colt and get into his SUV. Colt has a Land Rover, a red one he fixes himself. The vehicle runs like a dream and the inside has dark blue leather seats he custom fitted in here. They're even heated.

"Urgh, I wish I had your car," I say, as I snuggle down in the seat and clip my seat belt on.

"I would give you anything, Harper, but not my car." He winks at me and I laugh. Colt makes sure his seatbelt is latched before turning on the car to drive us the ten minutes out of town. I smile and lean back in my seat when I see where he is driving us to.

"The water tower?" I ask him.

"Where else? We always go there when we want to be alone," Colt says, and I turn the heat on for the seats.

"Alright, anything is better than going back home," I comment.

"What did she say?" Colt asks, picking up straight away that my foster parent has done something.

"The usual; she wants me to move out, but it's still difficult to hear on your eighteenth birthday, you know?" I try not to think of my foster mum and how she needs me to move out, as she doesn't get paid to look after me anymore. Every foster home I've been in has been about the money, and they want a child that they basically don't have to deal with. There isn't one I can remember being loving. I've been in foster care for as long as I remember, since I lost both my parents, but I was too young to remember their deaths. I don't even have photos, or anything from them, as it was all sold or lost over the years. I wonder if I look like them as I see my reflection in the window; my big green eyes, my long brown hair, and my golden skin. *I wonder what parts of my face look like my mum or dad?*

"You could come and live with me," Colt tells me, snapping me out of my thoughts.

"I'm sure your parents would *love* that. They don't like me, remember?" I chuckle.

"They don't get you, it's not that they don't like you. I can't explain it, but trust me, they wouldn't say no. I won't see you out on the streets, Harper," he says, resting his hand on my knee for a second and squeezing it.

"I know you wouldn't." I smile at him as he returns his hand to the wheel. Colton pulls onto the old road, where the water tower sits at the end. The tall fixture hasn't been used in years; it was just left here, and looks like it's close to falling apart. Colton parks, and I get out, following him up the pathway that is made of crumbling stone and weeds. He doesn't have to worry about the car being stolen around here, as no one comes this far out, so he doesn't lock it. I climb up the old ladder that has bars around it to stop people falling, and pull myself onto the circular walkway near the top. I wait for Colton to climb up before we go and sit on the edge. I hook my arms through the bars as my legs dangle off the side. I used to be scared of the height, but eventually, when I started to look around at the town, and the lights, that fear dissipated. It's better not to let the fear of falling stop you from seeing the beauty of where you are.

"I like it when you watch the town; your whole face lights up," Colton tells me. I turn my head to look at him as he takes a piece of my brown hair in his fingers, twirling it gently before letting it fall.

"Colt," I whisper as he moves closer and pulls a box out of his pocket.

"It's your birthday gift. Well, the first one, and the second one, I'll have to give you tomorrow, as it's not done." I'm finding it hard to look away from him as he moves that bit closer to me.

"Oh. You didn't have to get me anything, but I'm not going to say no." I chuckle a little and accept the box. My eyes widen when I open it and see a bracelet inside. There are three silver crystals, shaped like roses, sitting in the middle of a silver bracelet.

"This is amazing, thank you so much," I tell

him as he takes the bracelet out the box for me. I offer him my wrist, and he ties the bracelet, then smiles at me.

"It's meant for you," he says, moving to brush a piece of my hair behind my ear. His face is so close to mine. When his finger trails down my cheek, to my neck as we stare at each other, my breath hitches. Colt has never touched me like this before.

"What are we doing, Colt?" I ask him. He starts to answer when his phone rings. The phone ringing ruins the moment between us and I move back. Colt swears under his breath as he gets his phone out of his pocket.

"Hello?" he answers as I lean back, and annoyance crosses his face.

"Yeah alright… alright… bye," he tells whoever is on the other end, and then ends the call.

"I have to go, but I'll drive you home first. Can we meet up tomorrow? There's something I really need to tell you," Colt says.

"Should I worry?" I laugh, and he shakes his head with a sad look. He goes to say something, but his phone rings again. He takes a deep breath as he stands, pulling me up with him.

"Not at all," he smiles. *Yet I can't seem to make myself believe him.*

CHAPTER TWO

HARPER

"One more drink. Come on, you're eighteen!" Skye shouts, clearly more drunk than I am. She grins at me as I accept the small shot that can hardly be called a drink. I down it quickly, feeling the liquid burn my throat. *It is my birthday, after all.* Skye wanders off into the party, happy with herself that I've had a drink and I'm relaxing a little. I look around the woods, seeing the huge fire in the middle of the clearing, and my drunk classmates that surround it dancing to the loud music. They clear as one guy I don't know kisses some random girl and everyone cheers. I watch as Skye talks to them all, and they laugh at whatever she says.

I prefer to sit in the corner quietly and I wish I could have brought my kindle with me, but Skye wouldn't allow it. All she's cared about since I got here was where Colton was. He was right; I should have stayed at home or went out with him, or something. This isn't what I would call fun, but I wanted to try what normal eighteen-year-olds are meant to be doing. My phone buzzes in my pocket and I pull it out, seeing my foster mum's name flashing on the screen. I stand up, pulling my red coat closer around myself as I walk away from the party, and answer the phone call.

"Harper, where are you?" she asks me straight-away in her annoyed tone. I'm honestly surprised she's noticed I'm missing; she usually never does.

"I'm out with friends. It's my birthday," I say, not feeling the need to explain anything to her anymore. She made it clear last night when she told me she isn't getting paid to have me anymore, she wants me out. I didn't get presents when I woke up; instead, I got told to make plans to find somewhere else to live. I don't know what I was expecting.

"You're not with that older boy, Colton?" she asks in an accusing tone.

"Colton is the same age as me, I've told you this millions of times, but no, he isn't here," I mutter. I don't know why, but she's convinced Colton is older than me when he isn't. It might have to do with how mature he is compared to most of the idiotic boys my age.

"I want you to come back home," she says, her voice quiet and extremely unlike the usual way she shouts at me. I keep walking through the woods, as I think about what to say to her. Miss Linderale is the fourth foster parent I've had, and honestly, one of the nicer ones of the bunch. The rest are not worth thinking about.

"I don't get you. Why do you want me home? What changed from this morning?"

"Nothing. I wish I could keep you living with me, but I can't afford to, Harper. I thought you could come home and we could look at local places for you to move to," she tells me, but I don't believe her for a second. Miss Linderale has a large three-bedroom house, and her husband works a good job. They have expensive things all around the house, and she never goes anywhere in any clothes that aren't designer. I know I should have applied to college, but I didn't have enough money, or the grades, because of moving all the time. You don't have time to study when you're packing your stuff, or hiding from the new weird foster parents the social workers have found.

"Colton said I could move in with him and his family," I respond, disappointed, knowing some deep part of me just wants to be accepted by her.

"You cannot do that, Harper. You know how strange his family is. They never invite anyone over to their house," she says.

"I've been over once, they aren't that bad," I tell her, only lying a little bit. They *are* weird and cold, but it's not like they actually said anything bad towards me.

"Harper, just come home so we can talk. I'm not a heartless woman. I want you somewhere safe and with a planned future," she tells me.

"Sure, I'll come home soon," I say, kicking a rock with my foot and watching it fall down a hill. I stop walking when I realise how far I've gone; so far that I can't hear the party music anymore. I turn around in a circle, looking for the fire, and see it in the distance. I start walking back as Miss Linderale goes on about being responsible and saying that she's going to wait up for me.

"Do you understand, Harper?" she finishes.

"Yes, I'll see you in a bit," I say and end the call before she can lecture me anymore. A deep, long growl comes from behind me and I turn, my eyes widening at the sight of a big black wolf crouched down not far away from me. The wolf growls again and then turns, running into the forest.

"Wait!" I shout before I even think about what I just said. The wolf stops, looking over its shoulder at me as I step forward. It can't be a wolf; this is England, and we don't have wolves here, so it must be someone's pet. I don't want to get too close, but I should take a photo to put on the town Facebook page, in case someone lost him. I take another step closer, pulling out my phone and keeping eye contact with the wolf. I quickly glance down to open my camera. The growling gets louder and I look up just in time to see the wolf running for me. I drop my phone and turn around, running as fast I can towards the party.

I shouldn't have done that. I can't believe how stupid I just was.

I scream when teeth clamp down on my leg and biting, and I slam onto the ground, my chin smacking against the hard dirt. The wolf pulls on my leg, ripping my skin as I scream and try to kick him off. It doesn't work and everything is going blurry as pain racks through my leg. The ache consumes every thought as I reach down and try to push the wolf's head away from my leg. All I can see is the blood on my hands and all over its face, mixing with its black fur and white sharp teeth. *It's going to kill me.*

"Help!" I shout, my words quieter than I want them to be. Nothing makes sense as the wolf shakes my leg and pain causes the words to choke in my mouth. As everything starts to go black and the forest disappears, I see a grey wolf running towards me through the trees.

Its terrifying growl is the last thing I hear.

CHAPTER THREE

COLTON

"Harper, answer your damn phone," I mutter as her phone rings and then goes to voicemail. I look around my bedroom, settling on the glass of blood on the side table and feel my teeth respond. I down the drink as I wait for the stupid beep. I run my hand through my hair, not even knowing what to say. I've already left her ten messages.

"I don't know where you are, but I know you didn't come home after the party. I called Skye, who said you walked off. I'm getting worried now. Call me back," I say and put the phone down. I first went to her foster parents this morning, and her foster mom said she moved out. I don't trust her as far as I can throw her. Harper wouldn't just disappear like that without saying something to me. Plus, she has nowhere to go. I walk out of my bedroom, stopping when I see my sister Belle talking to my other sister Light in the corridor. Belle is kneeling down, as Light is only eight and tiny. Both my sisters have the same colour blonde hair, like mine, and pale skin. Both very pretty and I know I will have trouble protecting Light when she is as old as Belle and has men chasing after her. Luckily for my dad and me, Belle isn't interested in dating and turns every man down. It's almost funny to see the same reaction from every guy.

"What was the bad dream about?" Belle asks Light.

"Wolves. A wolf bit a girl and then there was a war. A bad war, and you-" Light starts. As I step closer, she stops talking, giving me a sad little smile. I don't know what to say to her; Belle is the best with her, out of all of us. Light isn't my biological sister but she is a vampire, and she lives in our coven as my parents adopted her as a baby when she had no one left. The ten blue stars in a circular mark in the middle of her forehead puts her at risk.

"It's just a dream, it's not real," Belle tells her

and then stands up. "Why don't we go and make some of that fried chicken you like?"

"Okay," Light replies, and they walk down the stairs. I try to ring Harper once again as I let myself out of the house and get into my SUV. I hate that I can't be with her at night; not until I explained everything, and now this happens. It would freak her out to see my extended sharp teeth and glowing purple eyes. She is human, after all.

"Where are you going?" Belle asks, stopping next to my window, having run impossibly fast to the side of my Land Rover. I roll my window down, and she leans in, her long blonde hair sweeping the ledge. Her eyes, the same colour as mine, are hard to look at. She knows I'm worried.

"To find Harper. She isn't answering her phone, and that's not like her," I say.

"The human," Belle tuts. Belle hates humans, and wolves and well, everyone that isn't her. Except for Light, who grows at a normal human rate until she turns eighteen and has made Belle fall in love with her. I want to blame Belle and tell her to be less harsh to people, but she had a bad past.

"She is my destined mate, Belle. Mine. I knew it was her when I first saw her, but I was more certain than ever yesterday, on her eighteenth birthday.

What went from a slight desire, and a need to be close to her and protect her, turned to actual pain in my chest from being away from her. I will go mad if I lose her now, I can't," I reply.

"Okay, okay, chill…but I still think you can do better than her," she says, and stands up as I glare at her.

"You have never met your mate. You wouldn't be able to understand," I tell her, and she just shakes her head at me. Belle is my sister, but there are one hundred years between us, which makes her think she knows everything. Belle doesn't know anything about Harper because she never tried to get to know her. I haven't even told Harper about my siblings yet because I know she would want to meet them and they wouldn't behave.

"One more thing. There were rogue hunters in town last night," she says, and I groan. That's not a good sign. If hunters were here, then a rogue would have been in town. Rogues have no control of their wolves; they are basically wild animals. It's like a vampire who doesn't feed for three weeks – they go feral, attacking anything or anyone. I drive to where the party in the woods took place the night before, parking next to the bottles of beer and rubbish that is surrounding a deserted campfire. It takes me a few minutes to track Harper's scent and I run fast through the woods towards where the scent is strongest. I stop when I see the blood; there's so much blood. I can smell that's it's not all Harper's, that some of it belongs to a wolf. The rogue must have attacked her, but I don't see her or her body anywhere. I feel sick as I pull my phone out.

"Dad, I need your help. I need you to use your powers to find Harper," I beg. My dad can track anyone, and he only needs to meet them once. My father is an exception to the rules, a turned vampire with a gift. He once worked for the vampire royal family; now, he is retired, in a way. Or retired to protect Light, as he was the one who found her on the doorsteps of the royal castle as a newborn baby.

"Harper?" he asks, knowing I would never ask him for anything unless I had no choice.

"Yes, I think she's hurt," I say.

"I can see her in a car, with wolves. The wolves have a bag that says the Forest pack on it," my dad says eventually. "Be careful, the wolves won't give her up easily," he warns.

"Thank you," I reply, and end the call before he can try to convince me not to go after her. I run back to my car as I search the pack on the supernaturals website, and see that it's a large pack in Ireland.

"Seems like I'm rescuing my destined mate from some wolves," I mutter, as I get in the car and start the engine.

CHAPTER FOUR

HARPER

"Shit, you wake her. I'm not," a male voice says, as a bright light shines into my eyes and then disappears again. I mentally groan; my head is killing me and the light is annoying my eyes.

"We should wake her. We're going to be at the pack in ten minutes. She needs to be awake for that," a woman's voice says in reply as a hand shakes my shoulder. I blink my eyes open, pulling my head off the side of the car door where I was leaning, and look over into a pair of bright green eyes. They belong to a woman about my age, with long golden curly hair and doll-like features. She smiles widely, making her look even more innocent, but there's something else about her; it's in her eyes. She looks too old in them, older than she should be. I move a little in my seat, wincing at the pain in my leg, and then everything comes back in a rush. The wolf biting me and the grey wolf I saw running towards me. I look down at my leg, which is bandaged up, then at my clothes, which are the same as what I was wearing at the party, but the leggings are rolled up.

"Careful, I wouldn't move that leg if I was you. Until you shift, you won't be able to heal quickly. So that's going to be sore for a while," the girl says, turning my attention back to her. I feel around my pockets, pulling out my phone and trying to turn it on. I need to call Colton, but the battery is flat, and the screen has cracks all over it.

"It's flat; you've been out for five days. Here," the girl says, and offers me a chocolate chip muffin in a wrapper.

"Five days?" I ask, feeling the hunger overrunning any of my common sense and I rip the muffin open. I eat it as she watches me closely, like I'm going to attempt to jump out the window of the moving car. I stop eating the food when I realise I've been missing five days. Five days, and Colton isn't going to know where I've gone. My bracelet is still there, and I find my hand rubbing against the crystals.

"It always happens, and it's always five days. I think it's something to do with the shifter gene getting your body ready for your first shift. But no one really knows," she tells me.

"Shift?" I ask her, my voice sounding croaky.

"Let's just get the fucking awkward part out of the way, shall we? We are wolf shifters. You were bitten by a rogue we were hunting and you're going to shift tonight," the man driving the car says, and I look over at him. He has wavy blond hair that falls to his ears and his green eyes meet mine through the car mirror.

"Please ignore my twin. Erik is an insensitive idiot," the woman says, and hands me a bottle of water from her bag. I take it with a nod, as I try to process what he just said. *Wolf shifter. They must be joking.*

"Anyway, I'm Gold Maystone, but most people call me G." She offers me a hand, and I look at her wearily before shaking my head, and her hand drops.

"Are you joking or trying to make me look stupid? Wolf shifters?" I say, putting the water bottle in my lap after having a drink. I guess they could have poisoned it, but I don't see why they would bother now. They've clearly been looking after me for some reason.

"No joke, Wolfy," Erik says.

"Shut it," Gold snaps, and then smiles at me.

"I know this is a lot to take in and believe what I'm telling you, but it's true. Wolf shifters are one of many kinds, and it only takes one bite," she explains, as she pulls her white cardigan off.

"I was bitten when I was seventeen, three hundred years ago. A rogue took me, bit me, and then tried to make me his mate. Erik saved me but got bit himself doing so." She says and shows me a bite mark on her upper arm before pulling her cardigan back on. The bite mark is large and looks deep, a whiter colour than the rest of her pale skin, but it's clear what it is.

"This is all crazy." I lean back and remember how the wolf looked at me; how it seemed to get mad when I got my phone out. Colton isn't going to believe this when I tell him.

"Did you just say three hundred?" I ask her, and she nods, her blonde hair bouncing in front of her eyes. "So, you're immortal?"

"You are too. I mean, we can still be killed, but

other than that, we live for a long time," she replies, and I don't know how to process that or believe it. Everything she is saying feels like a haze.

"And you hunt rogues? You want me to believe that?" I ask her sarcastically, but she doesn't seem to pick up on it.

"Why wouldn't you?" she asks.

"No offence, but you look like a Barbie doll and as innocent as a kitten," I say flatly, and Erik laughs loudly. I watch as Gold whacks him on the arm, and he still keeps laughing.

"Looks can be deceiving." She winks, clearly not offended and has likely heard that one before.

"Where are you taking me?" I ask her carefully, after looking out the window at the trees we are driving through.

"To your new pack. Well, our pack," she says brightly.

"Where exactly is that?" I ask her first because there are so many questions for that reply.

"It's just outside a town called Lunaton. Which is in central Ireland," she says.

"You took me to Ireland?" I ask her, and she nods her head. Ireland is far away from Stratford-upon-Avon, where I was living. It's also so far away from Colton.

"Yes. We are the only Irish pack, and even though Gold and I aren't Irish, most the pack is," Erik answers.

"Pack?" I ask Gold instead of Erik. *That guy is strange*.

"The name of a big group of wolves that live together. My family, and now yours too. Wolves need to be near others, or they start to go mad. It's not natural for wolves not to be with others," she explains.

"So, the rogue who bit me?" I ask. It makes more sense that the wolf might have gone a little mad, with the way he attacked me. If there were a normal person inside that wolf, then that wouldn't have happened.

"Is dead," Erik says before Gold can say anything, and she hits him on the arm again.

"Rogues are exiled wolves, on the run from packs and humans. Wolves never leave packs of their own choice, and if they did, it would be a terrible decision. We have a royal family who you go to and change packs if there are issues and you want to move. Shifters can't be on their own long before their wolves end up taking over their human mind. The wolf in them literally kills them, and we hunt them down, making sure they don't hurt anyone," she tells me gently.

"You were too late this time. Someone did get hurt, and you've taken me from my life," I say, and she frowns, resting a hand on my arm.

"Maybe some things are meant to be. You didn't have anyone, and your foster mum had your bags packed at your home when we went there. She didn't even want to know where you were when I got the cash out to pay her off. She was a selfish human. You have a home now, and people who will be there for you." She moves her hand, leaning back in her seat.

"I had someone, and he will come for me." I frown at her confused look and look out the window again. I just have to find a way to tell Colton where I am because I can't believe it's meant for me to be away from him.

No matter if this was meant to be, how am I meant to accept it without Colton?

CHAPTER FIVE

HARPER

"Welcome to the Forest pack," Erik says as he stops the car outside a massive metal gate, which sits in the middle of an endless forest we have driven in for half an hour. I haven't said a word; just tried to turn my phone on, and glared at both Gold and Erik the whole time. Two people are standing next to the gate on each side, looking imposing and creepy. They both stare at us and then at each other, and I watch as the one on the left walks over to the car. The man is big, with a grey jacket and jeans on, and a serious expression as he looks at us.

"The Forest pack? Couldn't the owner or whatever think of a better name?" I ask Gold, who laughs.

"The alpha is the person who owns and runs the pack. He has three betas, and you are about to meet one. You have met my twin and me already. That's all three," she says, nodding at the beefy man coming over. Erik lowers the window, and the man leans in.

"New wolf?" he asks straightaway and he looks at me with a slight frown.

"Lewis, nice to see you again. Always a pleasure and yes, the rogue turned her before we got him," Erik replies.

"Alpha is not going to like this," Lewis says and straightens up, waving us in as the gates open.

"Why is the alpha not going to like me being here?" I ask.

"Erm…" Gold looks away, not answering my question. *That's not worrying at all.* I mentally curse and look out the window as we drive past more trees and down a dirt road. *The large jeep makes some sense now.* The dirt road opens up to a massive house, which looks like five houses combined. It's made of grey stone, with massive towers on each side that cut short of the giant trees. There is a large garage built onto the far side, with ten cars parked outside. There's a space between them, and Erik pulls the jeep into it.

"Let us do the talking and don't be scared," Gold says with a smile as she gets out the car. Erik doesn't say a word, just opening his door and walking away. I get myself out the car, flinching with pain when I stand on my leg. *That bloody hurts.*

"Here." Gold comes to my side of the car and puts her arm around me, letting me lean on her as we walk slowly towards the house, every step shooting pain through my leg. The house looks even more prominent when we get to the door and Erik pushes it open. He holds the door for us as we walk up the two steps and into the house. The inside is massive and I have a feeling every room is like that. The room has light wooden floors and a large staircase that curves around the wall with a long corridor full of doors underneath it. The one wall is stripped of plaster and polished, showing off the grey stone. *It's really nice.*

"This way; he'll be in his office," Gold says, leading me straight down the corridor in front of us.

"He never leaves the damn place," Erik mutters, and I see Gold glare at him.

"Shouldn't you go and see Snow and Arisa?" she snaps, and he looks away. *Who are they?* I don't have time to ponder their identities as we reach the second door down, and Gold knocks three times.

A deep, seductive voice responds, "Come in."

"Let me go and explain things to him a little," Erik suggests and Gold nods, stepping back to let Erik through. The door is left open a little, so I can hear what they say.

"What's wrong?" the man asks.

"The rogue we followed, he bit a human just before we got there. The buggar was hard to track," Erik says, and there's silence in the room for a long time. I look up, and Gold places a finger against her lips.

"The turned? Is the human alive?" the man replies after the pause.

"Yes, and we brought her here. She woke up today. We were lucky; she just turned eighteen and was a foster kid. The foster parent grabbed the money before we even had a chance to explain Harper is okay. No one will miss or follow her," Erik replies, and I look away from the door when I see Gold giving me a sympathetic look. Colton will miss me, and he will want to know where I've gone.

"Bring her in. We will have to sort something out," the man says.

Gold lets me go a little and takes my hand in

hers, before opening the door. I walk in, following her, and stop in my tracks when the man sitting behind the desk stands up as his blue eyes meet mine.

"Mate," he breathes out in apparent shock.

Mate?

CHAPTER SIX

HARPER

"What? No way…" Erik says in surprise as he moves next to us, but I can't look away from the man in front of me. He has wavy black hair, a slight five o'clock shadow, and bright blue eyes that almost glow. When he leans on the desk, watching me as I watch him, my eyes are drawn to the way his black jumper stretches around his muscular chest and arms. I can just see the tips of his jeans, and as I look back up to his eyes, I would guess him only a little older than me.

"What's your name?" he asks me, his words

making me shiver in the warm room. He seems to know he has an effect on me, as he smirks.

"Harper Smithson. Yours?" I say, as I stand straighter and cross my arms, ignoring the pain in my leg the best I can. I see both the twins look between us, but they don't say a word.

"Nikoli Forest," he replies, standing up and walking around the desk. He stops right in front of me, and I don't move a muscle as he places his hand on my upper arm. There's something in his gaze, the way he looks at me like he just found a treasure he had been looking for, for years, and it makes me want to stay still. I know it means a lot to him only to touch my arm, but I'm not sure why.

"You called me your mate. What did that mean?" I ask, and he smiles, making him look even more attractive than should be allowed.

"Male wolves are only destined for one, and the male can tell from eye contact with the female they are destined for," he tells me, moving even closer, so all I can smell is him and the forest-like scent that he seems to have. *It's sweet and strangely comforting. I didn't even know I liked the forest.*

"And you think I'm destined for you?" I ask eventually.

"Yes," he merely says, like its nothing, and I shrug his hand away.

"I'm not anyone's, and don't expect that I'm going to be yours just because you say I am. I don't even know you," I tell him firmly, which only seems to make him chuckle. I step back, flinching when the pain goes up my leg.

"You're hurt," he states, a small growling noise following his words.

"She was bitten by the rogue, remember?" Gold tells Nikoli. "He nearly tore her leg off. It's healed; well, almost. I checked it five hours ago, but she could still use seeing Tam to make sure it doesn't scar like mine," Gold says, and Nikoli nods.

"I'll take her," he replies, staring at my leg like he can see through the bandage or something. Or he can will the cut to heal with a staring contest.

"Wait, who is Tam?" I ask him as he steps away.

"The pack healer; it's a special gift. Turned wolves cannot get gifts, but those born as wolves receive gifts from their family line," he tells me.

"Right," I reply, looking at Gold, who gives me a small, encouraging smile.

"Can you walk, or do you need me to carry you?" Nikoli asks me and I give him a look that suggests where he can shove that idea.

"I can walk," I bite out. This is all too much, and most of me wants to run away from him, from this place. Another part of me feels safe here, and I shouldn't. I need to find Colton and get away from the man in front of me, who is looking at me like I belong to him or something. I mean, these people have basically kidnapped me and told me a load of fairy tales that I'm expected to believe. *Who believes in fairy tales anyway?*

"We won't hurt you. If you give us a chance and stay in my pack, you will have a safe home. I'm not expecting *anything* from you," Nikoli says gently, watching me like I'm about to run. It's strange that I can see that he knows what I want to do.

"Okay, but I want to speak to an old friend. I just disappeared on him," I say, and he nods, walking to the door and holding it open.

"I will sort out a way for you to contact him after we have looked at your leg," he tells me. Gold puts her arm around me, and I let her lead me out. We follow Nikoli down the corridor and I look back to see Erik walking away towards the front door.

"Go and see Arisa, at least, if not Snow," Gold shouts, my eyes widening in shock when he suddenly glimmers slightly and shifts into a giant grey wolf, like the wolf I saw before I passed out, and runs out the open front door.

I can't avoid or deny this anymore; shifters are real.

CHAPTER SEVEN

NIKOLI

"This way," I say, holding the door to the infirmary open and watch as Harper looks up at me wearily before she goes in. She doesn't trust me, and I don't blame her. Harper's long chestnut coloured hair falls down her back, and when she moves, it floats around her. I can't stop staring at her, the woman I've waited so long for, and she is more than I could have imagined. She is strong because even though she is in pain, she tries not to show it with every step. Stubborn too, and I have a feeling I'm going to have my hands full with this one. I've waited years for a mate, many more years than others would have. I've met hundreds of female wolves over the years, and it was always expected that I would mate with a born wolf. Not that turned are less powerful, they just don't come with gifts, and there aren't a lot of alphas that are mated to them. I don't care about any of those politics, though, and never have. I don't run my pack by the rules the royals set. Harper turns slightly to look up at me as she stops in the middle of the room, those warm green eyes locking onto mine, and I have the feeling she is looking for any excuse to run. I don't know her, but I know she doesn't want to be here. I don't blame her; she has had quite the introduction to the shifter world by being bitten by a rogue. I wish that rogues didn't turn as many innocents like her that they do, but it happens all the time. Harper is lucky that the twins found her and brought her back here. Hunters usually have to take newly turned wolves to the royal family and they have to attend the royal school to learn how to control their wolf. Not a lot of alphas will take in new wolves because they don't have time to manage and teach one.

"This way." I wave a hand towards the doctor's room, holding the door open. I watch as Gold nods with a smile as she looks at Harper and me. She and her brother hunt rogues for my pack, as well as two other pairs that go out, if needed, and they take jobs for the royal family because they pay so well. My pack has seventy wolves and is small compared to some of the packs around the world, but it's still illegal to turn humans. We don't do that, and I will have to send a letter to the royals to explain what happened with Harper.

"Who's this?" Tam says as I pull the door shut behind the girls. Gold leads Harper over to one of the beds in the room, and she sits down. Tam is a little shorter than me with dark brown hair cut short and he always wears casual shirts with quotes on them. The one he has on at the moment is a picture of a grumpy looking cat and the words 'I'm not impressed' under it. The man is strange to me, but I like him. He has a class of three wolves he teaches healing to and overall, he is amazing at calming down wolves when accidents happen. I've never seen him not be able to find a way to heal anyone. The pack and I couldn't do any of the things we do without him.

"Tam, this is our newest pack member, Harper," I introduce, and Tam grins at me. I've known Tam since we were both pups, and he is one of my closest friends. There's no one else I would trust to heal her, and while I wish I could do it, that's not my gift. I have the power to calm someone down with one touch, which is good for an alpha to have when I have to sort out fights in the pack. I wish to use my calming power on Harper to help her relax, but mates cannot use their skills on each other. They dull each other out and its always been that way. I guess it's a natural thing, to never be able to hurt or control your mate.

"Hello, pretty lady," Tam says, walking over to her as Gold waves and sits down next to Harper. I smirk when Harper gives him a snarky look with a raised eyebrow. Tam looks at her in surprise; I'm sure he's shocked that his charms don't work on someone for once. Tam has half the women in the pack in love with him, and a string of one-night stands in the local town to prove how he always makes women like him. I don't have time for that; well, not until I saw Harper. I hope she gives me the chance to get to know her.

"Right… well, let's have a look at that leg you're limping on," he says, going to his knees and undoing the bandage. When I see the nasty bite on her leg, I grit my teeth, finding myself extremely glad this rogue is already dead, so I don't have to kill him myself. The rogue looked like he attempted to rip her whole leg off, with the ten or so bites I can see. It's started to heal but still looks terrible. I'm shocked that she walked in here.

"So, Harper, I'm going to place my hand on your wound, and it will feel freezing for a minute while I heal you. Just don't move, okay?" he instructs, hovering his hand over the central part of the bite. She nods, and I step forward on instinct when she screams as he places his hand roughly on her bite. A low growl comes out, and Harper looks over at me as pain rockets over her eyes. I walk over, taking her hand in mine as she bravely lets Tam heal her. It always hurts a lot, but it's over quickly. Tam leans back as he moves his hand away, looking at her leg, which is healed and only a little-dried blood is left there.

"That's amazing," she says looking down at her leg. "Thank you." It's incredible how there are no scars, not a bite mark in sight. I wish every wolf that is turned could see Tam or a healer like him. The scar that is usually left is horrible.

"No problem," Tam says, looking at my hand in hers, and he smirks at me as he guesses who she is.

"Congrats, old man. It's been, what, two hundred years of waiting?" he asks, and Harper responds.

"Two hundred? You're over two hundred years

old?" she asks me, removing her hand from mine, and I glare at Tam before nodding at her.

"Wow," she says, pulling her leggings down her one leg and standing up.

"I told you we live a long time," Gold tells her softly.

"I know, it's just…" she says, and Gold takes her hand in hers.

"I'm going to show Harper around and then find her room," she says, and as much as I don't want to be away from her, I know she needs a friend like Gold to help her settle in.

"She can have the one next to mine," I say, and Harper glares at me.

"I don't know what you expect from me, but that's not happening… I want a room away from you."

"It's safer for you to be near me, while you learn to control your wolf. I'm not expecting anything, but I want to keep an eye on you. You don't want to shift in your sleep and go running out of the house without me there to protect you," I tell her. It's happened more than once to turned shifters, and then they are away from other wolves for too long as their pack tries to find them. Their wolf takes over and then they are lost. It's a horrible side effect of the life we have.

"I won't ever be yours, you know that? This is pointless." She crosses her arms and glares up at me.

"Run all you want, Harper, but wolves love the chase," I reply, and her bright green eyes widen in shock. I turn around and walk out the room, knowing she is watching me. I have to make a plan to win her over.

CHAPTER EIGHT

HARPER

"So, this is the kitchen," Gold says as she opens one of the big glass doors at the end of the corridor, which opens into a large modern kitchen. It has dozens of cabinets, two large fridges and freezers, and a large double oven. All of the house is quite modern and clean; very clean for the number of people that live in it. I've seen several people walking around who have waved at us. They all have thick Irish accents, much like Tam has. Nikoli has a little accent, but it's not there that much, just the way he says certain words. I keep my eyes on the doors, seeing there's one in the kitchen, and one at the end of the corridor that leads outside.

"The pack always eats together, so we need a big kitchen. Come on." She gestures for me to follow her and walks back out the door. I follow her down the incredibly long corridor, and she opens a wooden door halfway down.

"How is everything so clean?"

"We have a rota for everything and a WhatsApp group chat, and everyone is on it. You will be added to help. It works well," she tells me. That's the strangest group chat I could ever think of.

"This is the living room," she says and walks in. I follow her, and the first thing I see are the four young women seated on two sofas in the room, watching a movie. One with long black hair pauses the film, and all of them turn to stare.

"Everyone, this is Harper, your new pack member," Gold says, introducing us. The one with black hair and bright blue eyes stands up, walking over. She is stunning – like, supermodel stunning – and I find myself staring. She also looks slightly familiar. She offers me a hand, and I shake it as she speaks.

"Nice to meet you, Harper. I'm Snow," she says.

I ignore the strange names they all have and simply nod. *This is just like a damn twisted fairy tale.*

"That's Sarah, Phoebe, and Daisy," Snow introduces the other women in the room and I wave, feeling awkward as Snow pulls Gold into a hug.

"How is my niece?" Gold asks her as she pulls away.

"Out at dancing class with the humans. I'm picking her up in an hour," Snow says gently.

"I can't wait to see her," Gold says, with genuine excitement in her eyes.

"It's good to see you, and she will be so happy. Is Erik back?" she asks Gold, who nods. A brief look of sadness drifts over Snow's face before she hides it with a big smile.

"See you later. I'm showing Harper around," Gold says, giving Snow a sympathetic look. I don't get what is going on there, but the girls on the sofa all give each other and Snow sad smiles.

"Every Friday, we have girls' night in here. No boys allowed and you're more than welcome to come. It's in three days and might be a good way to settle in," Snow tells me.

"Thanks, I'll think about it," I say, leaving out the fact I plan to leave here before then. She smiles, walking back to the sofa, where the other girls are watching me with curious faces. None of them looks unfriendly but growing up in foster care taught me not to judge people on their looks. The most innocent-looking person could be the cruellest, whereas the evilest-looking, could be the kindest.

"So, all down here are different social rooms. There is a game room, two offices, two studies, an art room, and the rest are mainly sofa-filled rooms for the pack," Gold explains as we walk out the room and into the corridor. I follow her back towards the entrance, stopping to stare when two men walk in through the doors. They stop as well, looking me over.

"Stop staring, it's not like we don't get new pack members. Don't you all have a job to be doing?" Gold says, and they give her an amused look before glancing over at me once more, then turn to leave.

"It will get better," Gold tells me.

"How many people live here?" I ask as we walk up the stairs.

"Seventy live on the lands. In the house, there are only ten that are invited to live here. The betas, the alpha, and his family. And a few wolves who are needed to be close to the alpha, like Tam," she says. I guess it makes sense to have the healer in the main house.

"His family?" I ask her. It suddenly hits me that Nikoli might have a girlfriend, and maybe even children. *Why does that thought make me want to be sick?*

"Yes. Snow is his sister, and she is married to Erik, with a child," Gold says, and some kind of relief fills me. I don't want to think about why I'm so relieved, so I settle on looking at the first floor we walk up to. There are many doors randomly placed down the corridor, and it's kind of empty, other than a cabinet and bookcase that I can see.

"This is my floor, and the others. You're up here," Gold says, continuing to walk up another set of stairs to the next floor. I follow her up, stopping to look out a massive window that overlooks the vast forest behind the house. The glass is stained with pinks and yellows, but it's still easy to see out of.

"We own about two hundred acres around the house. In the woods, are seven houses that we built over the years, and the other members of the pack live in them. When you shift, the woods are good to run and hunt in. The humans in the town have just gotten used to seeing wolves in the woods, and ignoring them," she tells me.

"When will I shift?" I ask her, wondering how close the movies I watched got to the real deal. I also know I need to shift first before I try and leave.

I just hope what they said about my wolf taking over doesn't come true before I can get to Colton and explain everything. I know I will have to return here, but I can't leave Colton just wondering where I am.

"Tonight. It's always the night after you wake up from being bitten. No one knows why again, but sometime tonight, you will shift. Nikoli will take you out to the woods and help you. You need an alpha around," she says, and I pull my gaze away from the woods to look at her.

"Why can't you?" I ask, not wanting to be alone with Nikoli.

"I'm not an alpha, and I couldn't control you if you need help," she laughs, but stops at my worried expression. "He makes you nervous, and that's normal. But, come on. Nikoli is one fine-looking guy," she says, knocking my shoulder, and I laugh.

"He may be a little bit attractive," I say, and Gold raises her eyebrows at me. I shake my head at her and start thinking of his soft-looking black hair and fantastic body. Attractive is a significant understatement; the man seems like everything a woman could want. I haven't dated anyone in a year, and even then, it was some stupid guy that only cared about feeling me up, and I ended up slapping him. I met Colton not long after, and no guys would come near me, as they assumed I was dating him. Gold doesn't reply, only laughs again as she carries on walking up the stairs. I follow her up and at the top is another corridor with three doors. Straight in front are two double doors, and two single ones next to it. Gold walks over to the only door on the left and opens it. I walk in as she holds the door open. The room is lovely and simple, but more than I've ever had before. It's way too big and nice.

"I can't accept this room. It's huge," I say and Gold chuckles.

"He isn't going to want his mate sleeping far away from him, and the *house* is huge," Gold says, and I suppose she is right.

"Look, get some rest, and Nikoli will come to get you later. If you need anything, I'm going to be in the gym, which is at the back of the house."

"Thank you," I tell her, and she nods, understanding what I mean.

CHAPTER NINE

HARPER

"Can I come in?" Nikoli's voice comes from the other side of the door, seconds after he knocks twice. I sit up on the bed straightening my hair from my nap.

"Sure," I call back, and he opens the door, walking in. Nikoli stops when he sees me and smiles as he looks me over. Nikoli has a jumper on, and tight jeans that I find myself not being able to look away from.

"Did you sleep well?" he asks.

"Yeah, great. Well, not so great… with the whole 'turning into a wolf' thing coming up," I admit, looking out the big window at the moon in the sky. I wonder if the moon has anything to do with wolves, like fairy tales usually say.

"We should walk to the woods. Turning inside the house wouldn't be a good idea," Nikoli says, diverting my attention from the window to him.

"I don't have a coat or anything with me to wear," I reply, and he nods his head at the rucksack on the floor by the door. It wasn't there earlier, so someone must have put it in here, or he could have brought it in while I was sleeping. My red coat is lying on top of it, and I pull my shoes on before walking over to it. I pull the red coat on, ignoring how it reminds me of the wolf that bit me. I can't see any blood on it, but the memories don't leave me. I think I hate this coat.

"Tell me about yourself," Nikoli asks me, as he holds the door open. I walk out and towards the stairs.

"I'm eighteen, and used to live in Stratford-upon-Avon. My parents died in a house fire when I was two. I was rescued, and then I lived in foster care until now." I tell him the simple things; things he could find out by just searching me on Facebook.

"I'm sorry about your parents. I lost both of mine as well," he says, but it does shock me a little. I've never met anyone who has lost their parents like me. Even in foster care, the other children are usually given up or don't speak about their pasts.

"How?" I ask, and he looks at me for a second before carrying on walking down the bottom staircase.

"There are other shifters, and we don't get along. There was a fight for this territory when I was five, and my parents died making sure me and my sister could escape," he explains, a tad of emotion lacing his words. I get the feeling he doesn't speak about his past often, or at all.

"That's terrible," I say gently.

"Yes, but the other shifters paid for their mistake; for stealing our land and killing our parents. I grew up and took everything my parents lost back," he tells me. I wonder how long that must have taken him and how determined he must have been to come back here. I watch him as we reach the end of the staircase and continue down the silent corridor. I would undoubtedly use "determined" as a word to describe him.

"What other shifters are there, then?" I ask.

"Wolves and bears are the most common around here. There's a bear shifter pack on the border of our lands, actually. When you go into the local town, you might meet some, and we have an alliance with them. Actually, I would consider the three alphas friends," he comments.

"So just wolves and bears?" I ask, and he chuckles as we get to the end of the corridor. He opens the back door and leads me outside. I pull my coat closer as the cold wind hits me and makes me feel freezing.

"No. There are a lot of different shifters. We even have a different shifter in our pack, a tiger. Cats and wolves don't usually get along, but I found Evlan in the foster system as a child. My friend works as a social carer and tells me if there are any unusual reportings."

"Like a child turning into a tiger, I'm guessing?" I ask.

"Exactly. He shifted and ran off. I found him and then adopted him. Tigers are rare, and I was worried he wouldn't fit in with the pack, but he did. Evlan is mated to one of our wolves, and they even have a baby on the way now," he tells me. It's clear how proud he is; I can hear it in his voice.

"You say our pack like it's mine also, when it isn't," I state, as we get to the trees. Nikoli slides his warm hand into mine, and I freeze, not sure if I should pull away from him.

"Because it *is* ours. You're my mate, and I'm

alpha. You are the alpha female of this pack now," he tells me. I go to respond when I feel pain in my stomach that takes my breath away. I wrap my arm around my waist as I fall to my knees.

"It's normal. The pain will fade, Harper. You have to let go and trust your wolf. She will never hurt you as she is part of you. She is part of who you are now." Nikoli's strong words come through the haze, moments before everything goes blurry. The first thing I notice is the warm feeling of my body and the way everything is in black and white as I open my eyes for a second before the colours of the forest and everything else slowly come back. A wolf is lying its massive black head on its paw in front of me. It tilts its head ever so slightly before I hear,

"Harper, your wolf is lovely. She is a deep brown, almost red, colour, with white-tipped ears."

"You can talk in my mind?" I reply to the deep voice of Nikoli. The wolf in front of me stands up, stretching.

"Yes. Let's run," Nikoli replies and the wolf walks closer, nudging me with its nose. It's strange to move for the first time in wolf form; it's like walking when you're drunk. I stand up a little, wobbling, and look down at the ground. I can see one brown

fur-covered paw and the ripped bits of my clothes all over the field. Well, at least the coat is gone. When I look up and back into the eyes of the black wolf, I know it's Nikoli. The glowing blue eyes are so like his. Nikoli nudges the side of my head with his and then turns around, running through some trees. My wolf runs after him, without me thinking about it or controlling my body. I can feel her, as she takes over a little, and I have a feeling she runs on instinct and not logic. I don't know how long we run for until we come across a river. My wolf drinks from the stream with Nikoli's and then sits back.

"We should go back, but you did well," Nikoli tells me.

"I did?" I ask.

"Perfect for an alpha female. You're perfect, and I'm so happy you're here. That you found your home," he tells me, and I stare over at him, seeing the bright blue eyes that look stunning, even on the wolf. We run back to the house, with me following Nikoli the whole way. He stops just outside the back door and I watch as he shifts back, his entire body faintly glowing grey, and then he is human again. The naked, perfect human body that I can't stop looking at.

"Shift back," he says, standing there, not one bit bothered by the fact I can see everything. Everything looks big, and I try to pull my eyes away from all the chiselled chest, and the happy trail that leads to a part of his body which is apparently delighted I'm here.

"Harper, to be human. You need to imagine it. Imagine your body," he tells me, apparently amused. I do as he asks, imagining my long dark hair and my round face. My green eyes and pale skin, and I feel my body moving. It's hard to explain what it feels like, other than a wave of heat caressing my body. When I open my eyes, I lift a hand in front of myself and see it's normal. *I'm back.*

"Here." Nikoli holds out a long shirt for me, and I quickly pull it over myself as he watches.

"Are you not going to put something on?" I ask him. He slowly looks me over, starting from my feet, up my legs, my stomach, and my breasts under the shirt, and then meets my eyes.

"No, Harper," he says and opens the door, walking in. I watch his fantastic ass as he walks down the corridor. *That's a view I wouldn't mind seeing often.*

CHAPTER TEN

HARPER

"Harper," I hear my name whispered, and I open my eyes to the dark bedroom, smelling something sweet and familiar. I turn my lamp on, holding in a scream when I see a shadow just outside the window. The shadows move, and I sit up in bed, turning my bedside lamp on to see better.

"Harper, come here. It's me." I recognise Colton's voice this time, and I sigh in relief. I knew I would see him again. I slide out of bed, running over to the window, and opening the latch. Colt has a black hoodie over his face and all black clothes, to blend in as it's obvious he snuck in here.

"What are you doing? How are you?" I ask, wondering how he even got up here, and how he even knew where I was? I never got the chance to tell him. My phone charger wasn't in my bag and Gold was asking around for me today, so I can charge it, and then get a new one in town. Colton jumps down from the window and closes it behind him, before pulling me to his chest. I breathe in the scent of him, which is so much stronger now than it's ever been; he smells just like mint and something sweet that I can't put my finger on. "I was going to call you, and asked to borrow Nikoli's phone; but he forgot, I think."

"Who is Nikoli? Is he the one that took you?"

"Took me? Wait, Colton, how are you here? I don't understand," I say, confusion spreading through my words, and he steps a little closer, further into the moonlight.

"I'm so sorry I wasn't there before the wolves took you. They had no right," Colton says, and I frown as I pull away a little.

"You know about wolves?" I ask, and then look up at his eyes. The light is dim in here, but I can't miss the fact his once blue eyes are bright purple, and he has two sharp teeth protruding from his mouth. I step away, and he lets me as I take him in.

I've never seen him like this, never at night, and I know he has been keeping something from me now. He knows about shifters, and he looks like he could be one of them. He can't be human with the way he looks, and it takes me a second to remember him as the playful Colton, who is my friend and would never hurt me.

"Colt, what's going on with your eyes and teeth?" I ask quietly, and he sighs, rubbing his face.

"We need to leave, and I can explain everything then," he says.

"I can't leave, not really. I'm a wolf now and I need a pack," I tell him, and he nods.

"I knew they had turned you, you smell too much like a wolf," he says, his voice deeper and scarier than before. "And no, you don't. You need to be around supernaturals of any kind. Being around me would stop your wolf from going mad."

"Being around you? What are you, Colt?" I whisper, and he steps forward, sliding his hand into my hair and moving that inch closer to me, so I have to lean my head back to look at him. His lips part to say something as the door behind me smashes open.

"Vampire, you chose the wrong pack to break into," Nikoli says behind me, walking into the room.

I step away from Colton, who moves in front of me. Don't vampires need to be invited into a house? Or maybe that's just because I watch too many vampire tv shows.

"You need to make your pack harder to break into. I just walked in. Lame for a pack this big," Colt laughs out, winding Nikoli up. *What the hell is he doing?*

"Don't worry, we keep stakes in our rooms for your kind," Nikoli says, and with speed I didn't know he could run, he charges into Colton, and they both fly out the window. It smashes to pieces as I tuck down and hold my hands over my head. The glass sprays all over me and the floor, as I listen to them thumping around and land outside.

"Nikoli, no!" I shout, running over the glass and screaming a little as bits cut into my feet. I suppress the pain the best I can, knowing that if I don't get down there quickly, they might kill each other. I pull myself through the broken window, trying to ignore the glass that cuts my arms. I look at my arm to see the cuts healing quickly and pushing the tiny bits of glass out of my skin. Just outside the window is a ledge, and below are Nikoli and Colton, beating the crap out of each other like I knew they would be. It's odd to see because they both move so fast with every hit, and neither of them pause as they fight back. I look down at the ground as I pull myself onto the ledge and know if they made that jump, I should be able to as well.

"Nothing to it, just jump," I tell myself, and then push off the ledge with a scream. *I don't like heights*. I roll when I hit the ground, hitting my side, surprised how it didn't hurt that much. I look up from the ground as Colton throws Nikoli across the grass. He lands smoothly and then gets up, smirking as he wipes some blood off his lip, and runs at Colton, landing a hard punch to his face, as Colton punches Nikoli's side. Neither of them seem to have noticed I'm even here. I look over to see Gold running out the door, Erik and another man I don't know at her side.

"Don't. Let me deal with this, but no one hurts the vampire," I shout at them, pulling myself up off the ground. They all look at me like I'm mad.

"Colton is a friend of mine, I can't let you hurt him. Let me stop them." The guys ignore me, but Gold pulls two daggers out of a holder on each of her thighs and raises them in front of Erik and the other guy.

"The alpha female will be listened to," Gold warns them and nods at me. "Go,"

"Nikoli! Colton, stop!" I shout at them as I run over. They both ignore me as they keep punching each other and rolling around on the ground. Both of them are covered in mud, grass and blood. Nikoli has blood all over his face as he holds Colton down on the ground and punches him hard enough to break something. Colton is holding him off, but I watch as Colton uses his legs to push Nikoli off him, and they both jump up into standing positions. I run over, stopping in the middle of them and hold my hands up. They both stop, staring at me, both making growling noises that would scare most people.

"Stop, both of you!" I shout, and they go quiet. Only the sound of our heavy breathing pierces the cold night.

"Colton is my friend. My only friend, and I trust him. I didn't know he was a vampire, and he is just upset because he thinks you took me," I tell Nikoli, who doesn't say a word as he stares at Colton.

"Colton, they didn't take me. Well, they did, but it was to help me. A rogue bit me, nearly killed me, and Nikoli's betas saved me. Nikoli has taken me into his pack and helped me shift. He isn't a bad person," I say, and Colton sighs, stepping close to me and sliding his hand into mine.

"Alright. I trust you if you say this idiot is a good person. You've always been a good judge of character," Colton says, and Nikoli growls.

"Do you want to say that to me again, Vampire?" He snarls. "In fact, get the hell out of my pack," Nikoli shouts in anger, and I sigh.

"Then we will leave, Harper," Colton says, stepping closer to me. His whole body is pressed against my back and his arm slides around my waist. I have no doubt Colton will pick me up and fight every wolf to get me out of here at this rate.

"She is my mate, and not going anywhere," Nikoli says, taking his own step closer to me, so close his whole body is pressed against my front. Both of them aren't looking at me as they stare each other down above my head. *Short girl problems right here.*

"Harper is *my* mate. I knew when I met her a year ago," Colton snaps.

"What?" I stare back at Colton as his words process through my mind.

"When we met, I knew you were my mate, Harper. I've known for a year," he says, gentler this time.

"Both of you, let me go. I need some space to process all this. Please," I ask them, and they both instantly step away as I think about what Colton is telling me. He is my mate, too. Another mate and I'm a wolf now; he is a vampire. It's like Twilight, but the jokey movie version of it.

"Why haven't you turned her yet? That makes no sense," Nikoli says, and Colton groans when he sees the look on my face. I don't know why I feel betrayed, like our friendship was nothing more than him thinking I belonged to him as a mate.

"I was going to give Harper a choice after she turned eighteen. I'm not like the rest of my kind; we don't force our mates to turn," Colton says, anger in his words.

"Didn't know you vampires even had any morals," Nikoli growls, and Colton moves closer, his chest brushing my hand that I automatically put out to stop him.

"Want to say that again, Wolf?" he spits out, his purple eyes glowing brighter in the dark night.

"Look, this isn't getting us anywhere. So, you both think I'm your mate, right?" I ask.

"Yes," they answer in unison.

"Well, what if I don't want to be either of your mates?" There's silence as I look between them. "Colton, you have lied to me, time and time again, since we met. I don't even know who you are," I whisper.

"You know who I am. Nothing about the year I spent with you was fake," he tells me.

"But it was based on a lie. And how do I know anything you told me was true? You're a vampire, from this world that I only just found out existed as I was thrown into it," I say gently. I don't want to think of any of our time as fake, it just couldn't have been. He was – is – my friend.

"Give me a chance. I will tell you everything about my kind. Anything you want," Colton says, stepping closer, and Nikoli growls louder behind me.

"Nikoli, I don't know you, but if you hurt Colton… I could never forgive you for that," I tell him, knowing if he ignores me now that he isn't the kind of mate I need; the type of person I could be with.

"I won't hurt him, not unless he hurts you. That's the only thing I wouldn't forgive," he assures me as his eyes lock with mine. I nod and give him a thankful expression.

"Tomorrow. I will come back here tomorrow, and we can go out. We need to talk. Alone," Colton says.

"You're not leaving this pack with him," Nikoli tells me, and I step away from Colton just to calm Nikoli down a little. I can feel how stressed he is from here.

"Nikoli, if this was the other way around and someone you thought was your mate was taken from you, wouldn't you do what Colton did?" I ask, his glowing blue eyes never leaving Colton.

"Yes," he answers eventually, like he doesn't want to admit it.

"Colton is part of my past, the only part I care about. Please don't take him from me or force me to choose right now." I move closer and place my hand on his arm. Nikoli seems to get some control over his wolf, as his eyes dim a little as he looks down at me.

"Fine. For now. You will need to choose, Harper. I will never trust a vampire with my mate," he tells me angrily and then walks off into the house, slamming the door. I feel like part of my heart breaks in that moment, and I hate he has that effect on me already. Gold, Erik, and the other man follow Nikoli into the house.

"Tomorrow at ten, I will come back." Colton steps closer when he sees how upset I am. "He is just angry."

I've never been able to hide how I'm feeling from him; he knows me too well. I don't move as he wraps an arm around me and hugs me.

"It's going to be okay, all of this," he says, but as I look at the door where Nikoli left through, I don't know if it is.

CHAPTER ELEVEN
COLTON

"**A**re you going to follow me all the way to the gate, or actually man up and speak to me?" I shout loudly, sensing Nikoli following me in the woods next to the path I'm walking down. The wolf never really left me alone with Harper; he was watching the whole time. I can tell that he will never leave us alone. He is too possessive, like all damn wolves. I can't get the look of shock on Harper's face out of my mind when I told her what I am. I spent a year planning a way to tell her without scaring her. I knew she was meant for my world because she is my destined mate, and that makes her destined for a supernatural life. Little did I know, she would become part of my world, without me even being able to hold her hand throughout it.

"Don't come back," he says as he steps out of the trees, his towering figure all I can see until he walks closer. I hear the slight growling coming from him; a warning, I suspect.

"That's never going to happen while Harper is here. It should be me that's mad; you stole her from me," I tell him, my own warning in my tone as my teeth naturally extend further than they usually are at night. It's not right that wolves and vampires are made out to hate each other in movies. No, I have no problem with wolf shifters, usually. Just this one that took my destined mate.

"She would have never had her life in danger if you actually protected her. A whole year being her friend, and the one time she needed you…you weren't there," Nikoli says, and I tighten my fists as I try to remember my promise to Harper. I won't kill the fucking wolf, but he has a point. I should have been there. I should have watched her from a distance or something, but no, I left her alone, and that's not a mistake I'm going to make again. I'm going to stay near, waiting and watching in case she needs me. I will never let my mate down again, and I don't need to justify myself to him.

"You're right, I should have been there. But she is mine, regardless. I won't let you steal her from me, wolf," I say, and the growling coming from him only increases as he takes a final step forward until he is inches away from me. We are the same height, our glowing eyes the only real light other than the moonlight shining through the trees.

"She doesn't want you, she hasn't left with you. It's clear where her home and heart is," Nikoli chuckles, and I lift my hand, punching him hard in the face. He swears before he hits me back and I duck, slamming my head into his stomach and smacking him into the ground. Nikoli hits me hard in the side, before grabbing my shirt and throwing me off him. I flip to stop my fall, landing and running at him again. I tackle him to the ground, noticing his arms going hairy, and I know he wants to shift. Nikoli wraps a rough hand around my throat, his nails cutting into my neck as I lift my hand and punch him again.

"Enough!" I hear someone say, but I'm too focused on beating the shit out the stupid wolf that stole my mate. I feel a hand pulling me off Nikoli just before I'm about to hit him again, and the person sends me flying, dislodging Nikoli's hand from my neck. His nails scrape across my skin, cutting deep enough to hurt, but I don't feel it as I'm only focused on ending this now. I land and stand up, seeing Nikoli get to his feet and lock his eyes with mine. A girl with long black hair steps in the middle of us. When I look at Nikoli and this woman, it's clear they are related somehow.

"Out of my way," Nikoli growls, trying to move around the woman, but she jumps in front of him and places her hand on his chest to stop him.

"No. You have waited years to find your mate, and I watched from the window as you fought with someone who is close to her. G told me she is his mate too. If you hurt him, there will be no going back from that, Nikoli," the woman warns him. "She would never trust you and would leave you. I can tell from the little I've seen and spoken to her, she cares deeply for those she loves."

"I can't share her with this little shit of a vampire, Snow," Nikoli growls out, his words just about understandable.

"Then you don't deserve her. Neither of you does, if you are out here fighting and not caring that every punch you throw hurts only Harper." Snow sighs. "Both of you are ungrateful. You know how long most people wait for their mate, a mate that can make you both happy?"

"Snow…" Nikoli starts to say, but she shakes her

head and steps away. Snow has a point. Many people wait so long for their destined mate and never find them. But it still doesn't make this easy to accept, to accept sharing Harper. I already love her, I have for a long time, and part of me feels like breaking when I see the way she looks at Nikoli. Another part of me knows it would kill her to leave him, and I never want to hurt her. *Talk about being between a rock and a hard place.*

"Kill each other if you want, or grow up," she says and then walks away. I lock eyes again with Nikoli, seeing he has calmed down a little, like I have, at her words.

"Leave, Vampire."

"You're a typical stubborn ass alpha, and you're not going to make this easy on any of us, are you?" I ask him. I don't wait for an answer as I turn my back on him and walk away. I walk to the gate, seeing two large wolves sitting on chairs, and one jumps up to open the gate when I get near.

"Thanks," I say, but neither of them replies as they look at each other. It's like they are daring each other to talk first, and it's almost funny. My phone rings as I walk down the road, towards my car parked at the end.

"Hello, sister," I answer.

"So…" Belle asks, not saying hello, but then she never does.

"It's more complicated than I thought. She is a wolf, the rogue turned her, and she has found another destined mate. The alpha," I say, and there's silence on the other end of the phone before Belle replies.

"Is she with you? Don't tell me the human chose a stranger over you?" she asks.

"She has stayed because she is a new wolf and needs to learn control. And she likes him," I add in, and Belle sighs deeply.

"Maybe you should leave her to it, find a new girl."

"There is no one else but her. She is my destined mate, Belle. I'm not giving up, even if I have to accept the wolf in her life."

"Do you really want half a mate?" she asks me, and it's a valid question. I know it will never be like it was before, with me having every bit of Harper's attention. But then, she was lonely. She needs something like this, a pack. *A family.*

"Better than no part of Harper," I whisper, as I get to my car and unlock it.

"Good luck then, brother, but I want to meet her. Bring her to the club," Belle says, and ends the call before I can tell her no. The club isn't my ideal plan for a first date, but then, it might be an excellent way to drive Harper into the world she is part of now. *A world that isn't just full of vampires and wolves.*

CHAPTER TWELVE

HARPER

"Y ou sure about this? He is a vampire,"
Gold says as she drives me to the gates
of the pack house, and parks the car
outside. I look over at Gold, who has a very sharp
looking dagger clipped to the side of her thigh, tiny
green shorts, and a long white top on. She looks like
Lara Croft, but blonde.

"Also, my best friend," I tell her.

"Just a friend?" she asks.

"He never tried to be anything more. I'm still in
shock that he thinks I'm his mate. We spent so
much time together, watching movies after school,
going swimming in the local pool every day in the

hot summer. But he never made a move. He never acted on anything he was feeling," I reply.

"What about what you were feeling?" she asks me.

"Honestly?" I ask, and she nods. "He was my friend, who I had a crush on, but never thought he would look at me like that. His parents are rich, he is stunning, and I was a foster kid with no money or future."

"I get it," Gold says gently.

"How can you?" I ask her, looking out the window.

"When I was about a hundred, I fell in love with a human man. He wasn't my mate, just a charming man, and we quickly became friends. He knew what I was, although he shouldn't have."

"Did he not feel the same way about you?" I ask.

"No, he told me one day that he loved me, but didn't want an immortal life. He also couldn't watch me never grow old, while he did. He wanted normal," Gold says, and pauses before continuing. "I left that day and went back twenty years later, just to see him once. He had a wife, two children, and he was happy." She gives me a small smile. "You're lucky. You both feel the same way about each other, and both will live long lives."

When she puts it like that, I know she has a point.

"Thank you for telling me that," I say.

"You're my friend," is all she says in response.

"It doesn't matter in the end. I can't have them both, and honestly, it would break me at this point to choose," I say with a sigh.

"It's normal for females to have more than one mate, but not across species," she tells me.

"So, neither of them would ever accept-" I start to say, but then I realise I haven't really thought about the idea of that, of them sharing me. *How would that even work? Could it work?*

"I don't know, Harper. But Nikoli has waited a long time for you. I feel he would do anything to be with you. What he said last night, he was just angry," Gold says sadly.

"He wouldn't even look at me as he passed me on the stairs this morning," I comment, and she sighs.

"I didn't say he wasn't a stubborn bastard," she chuckles. I open my door and step out when I see Colton's car pulling up to the gates, and Gold follows me over. The guards open the gates, both moving to stand on either side of Gold and me, as Colton gets out the car.

"Don't be too long. Remember the wolf that is here waiting for you," Gold whispers to me, and I nod at her before walking over to Colton.

"Hey," I say, feeling awkward, and he chuckles.

"Come on, I have a whole day planned for us," Colton says, and I don't say anything to him as I get in the car and put my seatbelt on. There's a weird silence between us as he drives through the trees and pulls into a small town. It has a shopping centre, a school, and a line of shops, but Colt drives past them all and parks in an empty space outside a zoo. The zoo isn't a big one, but I have never been to one before, and Colt knows that. I once told him how I wanted to go to a zoo and see the animals.

"You remembered," I say, leaning back in my seat and staring at the zoo entrance sign.

"Everything you told me, I remembered, Harper," he says.

"Why didn't you tell me what you are?" I ask him, and he turns the car off, both of us sitting in silence for a while.

"I wanted to. I really did, but I couldn't mate with you until you turned eighteen. It's against the supernatural rules. I knew if I told you…if I told you I had been falling in love with you since I first saw you tripping over thin air on the sidewalk and helping you stand up, there would be a chance you would want something between us, and I couldn't do that back then." The silence between us seems to grow as I think about what he is saying. Would I have wanted something more? Most likely, because if I'm honest with myself, I never just saw Colton as my best friend. He was always something more to me, but I could never admit that.

"There was a rock," I mutter the only response I can, and he laughs.

"No, there wasn't," he says, making me laugh too. I remember that day. He helped me up and introduced himself before walking off. Then he turned up at my school the next day, and everything else is history.

"What does it mean to be a vampire?" I ask him.

"I have to drink blood. Human blood, I need twice a week. If I feed on a vampire, I can go without feeding for two weeks because vampire blood is stronger. Although, I've only done that once, and it was from a glass at a bar," he tells me.

"Wolf blood?" I ask.

"Never tried it, but there are some of my kind

that hunt shifters for their blood. It's meant to be a power boost or something," he says, shaking his head. "I'm not like that, neither is any of my family, but I'm not going to sugarcoat the rest of my kind. They hunt humans, wolves, and other shifters for sport. Most vampires are evil."

I like that he doesn't hide anything about his kind from me. I wouldn't ever believe that he is like that anyway; he is too gentle and kind from what I know of him.

"How old are you? Nikoli is two hundred years old," I ask, knowing he could be any age and maybe what my foster parent said about him seeming older could be right.

"Only eighteen, that I never lied about. I'm a born vampire, both my parents are turned and with fay magic, I grow at a normal rate until I turned eighteen. Otherwise I would have grown a year older every ten years, it's a little complicated. I have one sister that is also born; she can talk to animals," he tells me.

"That's an amazing gift," I comment.

"It is. I never got a gift, but I'm stronger than any of my family, if that counts. And my dad is five hundred years old, and my mum isn't far off that," he chuckles, and I smile a little at him.

"Do vampires have a pack?" I ask him.

"It's called a Coven instead, and we have our own royal family. So do the fay and the elves," he tells me, and it's not even shocking me that there are other supernaturals now. Once you get used to the idea that you live in a fairy tale world, and that you're part of it, it all becomes normal.

"How many vampires are there in your coven?" I ask him.

"Just my family and one girl, who is seven, that we have taken in. My parents adopted her, so she is like a sister to me." He pauses. "Most vampires don't like how we live, and we have fought off a lot of them to stay alive,"

"I don't get it."

"We don't kill humans, we don't feed off them for a sport, like most our kind do. We have blood bags delivered. Most our kind think that's wrong, that everyone should follow the old ways," he explains.

"I'm sorry they are like that," I say, shaking my head.

"I don't see why they won't stop attacking humans; drinking from a bag isn't that bad."

"That's, well, a little gross, but you do eat normal food too. I've seen it," I comment.

"Yes, we can eat anything else we want." He nods with a small laugh.

"Why didn't you ever come out at night? Is that a vampire thing?"

"The glowing purple eyes and long teeth appear when it gets dark. I couldn't risk you seeing me like that," he says quietly, and I reach over, holding his hand like I always used to.

"The eyes were beautiful and unique. I didn't see the teeth, but I'm sure they just add to how good-looking you are, Colt," I whisper to him, and he tightens his grip on my hand.

"You're a wolf now; immortal, like me," he tells me firmly.

"Yes," I answer. I haven't really had time to process it yet – the idea of living forever – but I have to admit some small part of me is happy that Colt will always be at my side. That I won't have to watch him grow old.

"And still my destined mate," he says.

"And Nikoli's," I reply, just as calmly as his words were spoken to me.

"Harper, I don't know this wolf, but I know you. I can see it in your eyes; you feel something for him?" he asks me.

"Yes, but it's the same as I what I feel for you," I say quietly.

"Why don't we take it slow, all of us. If the wolf can deal with the fact I love you, then I can deal with the fact he is your destined mate. The fates wouldn't have brought us all together for no reason, Harper."

"You love me?" I murmur.

"I have for a long time. That's not something new," he affirms.

"You would do that for me? Deal with my feelings for Nikoli?"

"I would do anything for you," he tells me, and I can see the truth in his eyes.

"Where are you staying?" I ask him, desperate to change the subject, if only for a second.

"My family bought a house in town; all of them are here. I would like to take you to see them. They were only cold with you last time because they didn't know if I would ever tell you. If you would choose to stay human, and I would be alone for the rest of my life."

"They just want you happy?" I ask.

"Yes," he answers.

"I would like to meet them," I reply. If they were just protective of their son before, then I get it.

They must have been worried that I would end up friend zoning Colton or running away from him, if he told me he was a vampire.

"Next Tuesday?" he asks, and I nod.

"You know I had that gift for you, the one that wasn't ready yet?" he asks, and reaches inside his leather jacket, pulling out a picture. "Here." He hands me a photo of a couple holding a baby. The couple both have dark brown hair, and they are smiling down at the baby with a loving look.

"Who?" I ask, hoping for only one answer.

"Your parents. I found an old university friend of your mother's, and she sent me this. This was her wedding day, and your parents came with you. She gave me her number if you ever want to talk to her about your mum and dad, but she said she doesn't have any other photos that she knows about."

Tears fill my eyes as I look down at the couple, my parents, who seem so happy to be holding me. This is something I feel like I've waited for years for, and Colton did this for me.

"Thank you. I just-" I pause, wiping my eyes. "Thank you."

Colton doesn't say a word as he lets me stare at the photo for a long time.

"Okay, let's go and see some animals. I imagine

this is something they would have done with me as a child, and it's perfect that I have this with me as I go. It feels like a little bit of them are with me, even if they aren't," I say, and he nods his head.

"They are always with you, Harper. We live in a world full of supernaturals and magic. There's no way there isn't a chance that they could be watching you from somewhere. Making sure you are safe," he says softly, and then gets out the car before I can say a word. I don't know if I believe the same things as him, that my parents might be watching me from somewhere, but a little part of me hopes. I spend the next few hours with Colton, and in some ways, nothing has changed. He still holds my hand and makes me laugh, but there's something else now. It's the way we look at each other, and the way he smiles at me sometimes. One thing I know for sure; I don't want Colt out of my life.

CHAPTER THIRTEEN

HARPER

"This isn't fair. Just don't walk away again," I hear Snow plead as I stop mid-step on the second-floor stairs.

"I'm not walking away. I saw Arisa, gave her a kiss, and read her a story. What more do you want?" Erik replies bluntly. His tone is cold and I feel sorry for Snow.

"I don't know. For you to be my mate and be around more?" she replies quietly, but there's an edge to her words.

"I can't," he says, emotionless. I can't believe he is like this with Snow; she is lovely and sweet, the very opposite of Erik's cold nature.

"No, you can, but instead, you choose to go off hunting," she snaps.

"It's my *job*, Snow," he replies.

"No, you hunt rogues to forget about what happened," she says, and I hear Erik walking away, followed by the sounds of Snow sobbing. *What the hell was that about?* I wait until I hear Snow moving away before continuing down the stairs. I know she wouldn't appreciate me trying to comfort her at the moment, but I begin to wonder if they are destined mates at all.

"You took your time," Nikoli comments when I reach the back door, where he stands, smiling down at me. He slides his hand into mine and starts walking towards the forest.

"You seem happier today? Compared to how you were when Colt dropped me off," I say, and he grumbles something under his breath before answering me.

"I realised that I don't want to lose you. If that means putting up with the vampire for the time being, then fine. I can't promise I won't kill him if he touches you, but…"

"Nikoli, you can't kill him. He is- "

"Your destined mate too, I know. I'm trying, okay? I spent two hundred years waiting for you, and when I finally find you, you have another destined mate. It's a lot to deal with, Harper. My wolf doesn't like the idea of sharing you."

"I'm not asking you to share," I mumble.

"Yes, you are, you just haven't said it out loud yet. Sharing is normal for supernaturals, but not for a vampire and alpha wolf. I just don't know how it's going work." I don't know what to say to him other than repeat what Colton said.

"We should take everything slow. We are immortal and have plenty of time."

"I know, Harper," he says and squeezes my hand as I look away from him.

"Can I ask something? I know it's none of my business, so you don't have to tell me," I ask, and he nods.

"You can ask me anything. I won't keep anything from you, Harper," he replies, his words firm and almost demanding.

"So, Snow and Erik are mates, but they seem to hate each other. I don't understand why that is?"

Nikoli sighs. "Yes, they are destined mates, and have been together since Erik and Gold first joined the pack over a hundred years ago. They were madly in love and happy. Well, for a long time they were."

"What happened to them?"

"When Snow found out she was pregnant, they were over the moon with happiness. We didn't think she could have children, as it had been so long, and some wolves never do. When Tam told them that they were having twins, they couldn't have been happier," he says, stepping over a log of wood and offers me his hand to help me.

"One day, seven weeks earlier than the twins were meant to be here, Snow fell in the woods and broke her leg. The break kickstarted her labour, and Erik was away hunting for that week. I was there the whole time when she gave birth. It was a long and painful labour, as human pain relief doesn't work on wolves, and Tam couldn't heal her quick enough. When it was all over, her son died, despite how much we tried to save him. Arisa just about survived but the little boy, he was too small, too weak. The labour was too long and too early," Nikoli says sadly.

"Oh my God. Poor Snow and Erik," I whisper, having no idea how horrible that must have been for them.

"She was heartbroken, and when we finally got a message to Erik, and he came back, he couldn't cope with the fact he wasn't there. Losing one of their children broke them, and despite having Arisa, Erik just wanted to hunt rogues, and started taking more and more jobs from the royal family. He hunts for our pack sometimes, but he mainly works with the prince of the wolves, hunting."

"I understand why he feels guilty, but poor Arisa. She must not see her dad much," I comment.

"He tries with her, but I believe she is a reminder of the baby they lost too," he says, and I do understand that. It must be so hard.

"I hope that Snow and Erik can fix their relationship one day," I say gently.

"I highly doubt they can. Sometimes some things are too broken to be fixed."

"I don't believe that. I believe that everything is part of your fate," I tell him and step away, letting him watch as I throw my long shirt off and call my wolf. She responds instantly, taking over, and I blink my eyes open to see Nikoli looking down at me.

"Time to run, little wolf," he says, as he starts pulling his clothes off. I turn towards the forest and do just that.

CHAPTER FOURTEEN

HARPER

"What are you doing?" I hear Nikoli say behind me, making me jump and bang my head on the top of the cupboard I was looking through in the kitchen.

"Ouch!" I say, holding my head and leaning back from the counter before standing up to see Nikoli walking into the kitchen. I rub my head as he walks over, knowing my shifter healing will sort it out soon enough, but it still damn well hurts. Admittedly, I shouldn't be so quickly scared.

"Shit, I didn't mean to make you do that." He comes over to stand right in front of me. "Are you okay?" he asks, looking at my head.

"Yes," I chuckle, lowering my hand as he leans on the counter in front of me. I end up running my eyes over his white shirt, and very tight jeans. Those kinds of jeans shouldn't be allowed to be made or bought by someone like Nikoli. They look way too good; good enough that I can't keep my eyes off him. My wolf purrs in my mind, the same way she does when I'm around Colton too. She knows they are her destined mates, as well as mine.

"So…what were you looking for?" he asks with a slight laugh.

"The washing up liquid. It's my chore night, and I have to wash all this up. I can't find it," I say, and he laughs before walking over to the sink and lifting open the box on the window in front of it. He pulls out the washing liquid and smiles at me.

"Oh, right next to the sink. I should have guessed," I laugh.

"I will help. You have a lot, by the looks of it," he says, gesturing to the counters full of plates from the whole day. I didn't realise it was my day because I couldn't really understand the group chat message with the cracks on my phone. I didn't know what they wanted me to do, so I found Gold and asked her. By that point, there was a lot to be done.

"You don't have to," I say, walking over and taking the washing up liquid off him.

"I want to. You wash, and I will dry," he says as I turn the water on and add some liquid to the sink bowl. Nikoli gets a towel out of one of the drawers as I start washing the dishes.

"Do you like your room? is there anything you need?" he asks after a while.

"I love my room. I've never had a double bed before, and it's so comfy."

"I know you sleep well. You snore."

"I do not," I say, and flick some water at him. It drips down his shocked face, and then he bursts into laughter with me.

"Did you just flick me with water?" he asks through laughs.

"Yep," I say and do it again. He puts his plate down, puts his own hand into the water, and flicks it at me. We go back and forth until we are soaking wet and covered in bubbles, laughing our heads off. I end up running my eyes down his white shirt stuck to his chest, showing off his eight-pack and his hard chest. Nikoli could win any wet t-shirt contest, hands down.

"Okay…" I hear Snow say and we both stop,

looking towards where she is standing at the door with a big smile.

"Oh, hey, Snow," I say, wiping some bubbles out my eyes. Nikoli chuckles next to me and hands me his towel. He goes and gets himself another one as Snow heads to the fridge.

"Having fun with your chores?" Snow asks, as she gets a bottle of water from the fridge and closes the door.

"Nikoli was just helping me do the washing up, and then…"

"You both decided to have a bubble shower?" she asks with a laugh. I know my cheeks are going a little red.

"Something like that," Nikoli says behind me, and I turn in time to see him pull his shirt off, revealing the chest underneath that I was just admiring. It's not like I haven't seen him naked. I have many times after a shift, but it never seems to get old with Nikoli. All it does is make me want to go running with him, time and time again.

"I'm going to get some dry clothes before we carry on with this. Maybe you should do the same," Nikoli says, his eyes looking down at my own black tank top that is sticking to my body. At least it isn't white. I watch as he walks out the room.

"I haven't seen him this playful or having fun in so many years," Snow says once Nikoli is out of sight.

"I like him like this, so relaxed," I comment.

"It's because you're good for him," she states and walks out the room. It makes me wonder if Nikoli is good for me because, when I'm around him, he feels like home. The same way it feels with Colton.

CHAPTER FIFTEEN

HARPER

"So, you and Nikoli are getting close," Gold says, nudging me with her shoulder.

I wouldn't say close, just spending a lot of time together as he teaches me about my wolf. Nikoli has taken me out every night these last three days to shift and learn more. I've mainly spent days sleeping or eating in the kitchens alone because Nikoli gets busy sorting pack issues out. I haven't even seen Gold, until she opened my bedroom door a moment ago and walked in. I turn my phone off, a little upset that there is only one text from my old friend Skye, who congratulated me on getting into another foster home. She didn't sound suspicious at all, which is crap. *She apparently didn't care much about me.* I did have a chat with Colt, who is missing me and can't wait until Tuesday. It's strange being away from him this much, as we used to be together every day. I also listened to all his voice messages he left me, sounding so panicked when I went missing. They were hard to listen to because I could hear how worried he was.

"He is helping me learn how to be a wolf. Shifter control and all that," I say, and she laughs.

"You have more control than any wolf I've ever seen, and I highly doubt you couldn't control your wolf alone at this point," she says.

I reach down, feeling my wolf in my mind, and I know Gold is right. My wolf trusts me, as much as I trust her.

"It's girls' night, and you've been hiding in here all the time or with Nikoli. Come and meet some of your pack," she says, nudging me, and I frown at her.

"I forgot about that," I mutter, and she smiles.

"They aren't too bad, but they are interested to know more about their new pack member who has stolen the alpha's heart, and already has a vampire's," she says, as we stand up from the bed and walk towards the door.

"I haven't stolen anything," I say.

"You're so completely in denial, it's almost funny," she chides, laughing harder.

"Can I ask you something?" I ask her.

"Anything," she says, leaning against the wall by the door.

"Okay well, I've never been with a man, but I know how sex works. But is there anything I should know about wolves or vampires?" I say way too quickly, and she laughs when I finally stop speaking.

"Well, I'm assuming you guessed that to mate, you have to have sex?" she asks when she sees my blushing cheeks, and stops laughing. I can't stop thinking about mating with Nikoli and Colton but I need to be careful.

"Well, the male must bite the female during the mating for it to work. It's the same for vampires, but they have to exchange blood, I've heard. I would guess that you have to bite him hard enough to break the skin. But I've heard most of this comes from instinct," she explains.

"What about birth control?" I ask, not wanting to admit how happy it makes my wolf and me at the idea of mating with Nikoli or Colt.

"Wolves have trouble conceiving, and we have certain times of the year where our hormones go out of whack, and we need sex. That's the only time you can conceive. It's basically unheard of to conceive any other time," she says, and I nod, a little relieved.

"Do you have a mate?" I ask her. I also wonder what the females of the pack do when that time comes around, and you don't have a mate. I doubt many of them would be happy having a child with someone who isn't their mate.

"No. It's not common to find your destined mate, and most never do. Look at Snow. Even if you find your destined mate or mates, it doesn't mean you're going to be happy with them," she says, a hint of sadness in her words.

"How many mates could you have? I mean, I don't think I could cope with more mates turning up," I say with a chuckle, and she smiles.

"There isn't a limit on how many males can be destined for one woman. There is a woman called Daisy in the pack, who has four mates. They all live here and are happy together," she says gently.

"Wow. I can just about deal with one alpha, and one vampire, let alone anymore," I say, causing her to chuckle.

"You'll meet Daisy and her mates at Sunday dinner, and their son," she tells me.

"Who goes to that?" I ask, dreading her answer.

"The whole pack. It's the only time we all get together, other than meetings, which are rare."

"Have you ever dated anyone long-term?" I ask her, and she shakes her head.

"Some humans here and there but they grow old, and I can't tell them what I am. Eventually, it becomes easier to stay away from humans, as they die so easily and live so little," she says.

It makes me sad, in a way, that everyone I had in my old life, other than Colt, will eventually die, and I will still be here.

"What about dating wolves?" I ask her.

"And risk that they find their destined mate, then leave? No, I couldn't do that, and most wolves can't."

"Ah, I see," I say, and she nods sadly. It's not a great situation to be in for anyone, and it sounds lonely. So, part of me is glad that I met Nikoli when I did. I follow her out the room, and she gives me a small smile as we reach the bottom of the stairs. We walk down the corridor and back to the room where I first met the women, and Gold opens the door. I follow her in, and Snow walks over.

"I'm so happy my grumpy brother finally found his mate," she says and hugs me. I don't move as she attempts to squeeze me to death.

"We haven't mated or got together," I tell her, and she chuckles as she pulls away.

"Nikoli hasn't dated in years; he likely needs to work on his pickup skills. From what I saw in the kitchen, it won't be long," she says with a big grin, and I shake my head.

"Everyone, this is Harper. Nikoli's destined mate and our soon-to-be alpha female. I hope that you all will welcome her, and give the respect she deserves," Gold shouts into the room, and it goes quiet as all the women turn to look at me. A little girl, who looks about five, walks over and puts her hand out. She has curly black hair, a pale complexion, and bright green eyes, and is wearing cute fox pyjamas.

"I'm Arisa, and you're going to be my new auntie. We can have sleepovers and play dolls, and when you have your own baby, I will be its friend," she says, and I shake her hand, not knowing what else to do.

"Auntie?" I ask quietly, looking down at the little girl who is the image of Snow, but with Erik and

Gold's eyes. I guess this must be Snow and Erik's child.

"Yeah, we totally creeped you out now, but honestly, we are all just happy. This is my daughter," Snow says, and Arisa gives me an innocent smile as she pulls her hand away.

"What? Did I say something? I want her to have a baby, so I have someone to play with," Arisa says with a pout, and Snow laughs.

"Usually when you meet someone, you don't tell them to have a baby, Arisa. It's considered rude," Snow tells Arisa, who apparently thinks about it for a while.

"I don't get it. You tell me to always tell the truth, and I did," she says, and crosses her arms in annoyance. It's really hard not to laugh at her serious face; she is just too cute to pull it off.

"Come and sit down. We're about to put *Wonder Woman* on. The new one," Snow tells me, changing the subject. I ignore the looks of most the women in here as I follow Snow over to an empty sofa. Gold chooses to sit on the rug with another woman, and Snow plops down next to me. Arisa comes over and sits on the edge of the couch.

"No, it's bedtime for you," Snow tells her, and

she gives her another cute pout. I would have trouble saying no to that, but Snow doesn't.

"I mean it. I told you that you could meet Harper, but that's it. Your dad is waiting to put you to bed," she says. Arisa frowns, but gives her mum a hug before running out of the room.

"She is so sweet," a blonde-haired woman seated on another sofa says, and I nod.

"She is," another woman, with bright red curly hair, agrees from across the room. A very awkward silence fills the room as they all watch me for some kind of reaction. I look at Gold, who gives me a cheeky smile, but doesn't say anything.

"Let's watch the film. I've heard it's really good," I say into the silence of the room, and Snow winks at me as she gets the remote and presses play. It may have been awkward at the start of the night, but by the end, I made some new friends.

CHAPTER SIXTEEN

HARPER

"**N**ight guys, it was lovely to meet you all," I tell the room full of tired-looking women, and most of them smile at me as they say goodbye. I've been introduced to Catty, who is mated with four children, and she gave me lots of advice on children that made me want to run out the door. Then I met Melissa, a single wolf, who is training to be a hunter for the royal family after she lost her parents to rogues. Overall, most the wolves here have pasts, just like I do, and its shocking to find out how many of them were turned and not born wolves. It gives me some kind of understanding with them that I was in the same place they all were at some point when we were turned. They felt the same pain and fear. Gold and Snow wave goodbye as I leave the room, and my phone starts ringing. I get it out of my pocket and see Colton's name and the photo of him flashing. It's a silly photo really; just his goofy face, and the cracks in the screen make it hard for me to unlock the phone call.

"Late for a phone call," I answer, my tone playful.

"Not late for me," he replies, and laughs with me.

"What's up?" I ask him.

"Come to the gate and jump over it. The guards are sleeping, and I'm outside waiting for you," he says, just as I walk into the empty entrance hall.

"You can't be serious, and why are they sleeping?" I mutter, knowing that he is likely being *very* serious. This is Colt, my playful Colt.

"Come on, I want to take you somewhere. I even brought you clothes and slipped the guards some fey powder in their drinks, makes them a little sleepy for a while," he says, and I chuckle. I dread to know what clothes he bought me and how much effort he put into getting the guards to sleep.

"Nikoli would go mad if I left," I comment,

looking up the stairs, knowing he is sleeping up there.

"It's for one night, and he wouldn't know. I'll have you tucked back in bed by the morning. Promise," he says, boldly.

"Alright," I say, knowing part of me is desperate to see him and misses him. I walk around the house, to the door in the empty dining room I know isn't likely to have a guard on like the front door, and it's easier to sneak out. I run through the forest, towards the gate, keeping my ears open for anyone that could be following me. The freezing cold air makes my eyes water as I run, and I know I should have got a coat. It's too cold for escape plans without a jacket. I stop when I see the gate, slowing down, and see the guards are both sleeping in their chairs, like Colton said. I run as fast as I can towards the entrance and jump, flying over it and landing on the other side. I pause as one of the guards stirs a little in his chair, and then starts snoring again. I breathe out a sigh of relief.

I run away from the gate and down the road, smiling when I see Colton's car parked to the side, and he is leaning against the bonnet.

"Knew you could do it," he chuckles, standing up, and I find myself looking at him differently than

I ever have. Colton has black jeans, a white shirt and a leather jacket on. His blond hair is styled to the left, and when he pulls me into a hug when I get close, he smells amazing. I press my nose into his leather jacket, loving how the leather smell mixes with his mint-like smell. Nikoli, on the other hand, smells like the forest. Two things I never knew I loved the scent of until now.

"Are you smelling my jacket?" he chuckles next to my ear.

"What? Nope," I say, stepping back, and he laughs.

"Come on, my little sniffer, we have to get going," he says, and I shake my head at him as my cheeks grow warm. I get in the car at the same time Colton does, and he starts the car up as I slide my seatbelt on.

"Where are we going then?" I ask him as he drives through the forest.

"To a nightclub. A supernatural nightclub, to be exact."

It makes sense there are places you can go to meet other supernaturals, and a nightclub is indeed one way.

"Clubbing?" I ask him with wide eyes. I've never been or really had the chance to.

"You're eighteen, and everything has been so serious since your birthday. I want to get you out for a night." He shrugs a shoulder at me and smiles.

"I'm not dressed for clubbing," I look down at my black leggings and tank top. I didn't even get a chance to grab a coat. Not that I could wear a jacket into a club anyway.

"I bought you clothes, remember?" Colton says and stops the car. "Get in the back and get dressed. I won't look." He winks at me.

"I don't believe you."

"You're a wolf now. Aren't you meant to be okay with nudity?" he asks.

"You're so cheeky," I say with a laugh and climb in the backseat, while he carries on driving. I pick up the bag on the backseat and find the mini black dress inside, as well as some high heels. I roll my eyes. It's what a typical guy would buy, and I doubt there isn't going to be much on show tonight. But I don't want him to turn out and go home. I need a night out, Colt is right. I pull my top off and push my leggings down, only looking once at Colton to see he is still looking out the front window. I pull the dress on, which is a simple black dress that pushes up my breasts and stops around mid-thigh. It's very tight. I slip the heels on, surprised that he got my size right, and pull my hair out of the messy bun it was in, letting it fall down my shoulders. I keep my eye on Colton the whole time, but he never looks, like he promised he wouldn't.

"I'm climbing through again, but you don't need to stop the car," I say, and I see him nod before I climb over the seats. It's a little awkward, and I'm sure my butt is way too close to his head at one point, but I do get into my seat eventually. I look over to see Colton staring at me, not the road, and his eyes are lit up a brighter purple than they were before. This is the first time I've seen his teeth this close, as the sharp points just appear out of his mouth. I want to say part of me is scared – I *should* be afraid – but I'm not. No, I'm turned on instead, and can't stop thinking about how sexy he looks. How much I want to kiss him.

"Damn, Harper, I don't think I've ever seen anyone look as lovely as you do tonight," he says gently.

"Eyes on the road, Colt," I chuckle, and he smirks at me before doing as I ask. The drive is about twenty minutes to get into town and to the club on the other side. Colt parks in one of the empty spots opposite the club. The place looks deserted from the outside. And dodgy as hell.

"Really? It looks like a dive bar," I comment, looking at the place. It's what I can only describe as a hut, with broken windows and a door hanging off the hinges. There's trash all over the floor under the windows, and broken bottles lining the pathway to the hut.

"There's a fey glamour on the bar. It's amazing inside, but it looks like this to make humans avoid it," he tells me, then gets out the car. "It's perfectly safe here; it's a neutral zone. As in, no one is allowed to hurt another inside. There's magic that stops fights somehow, but I've never even seen a fight break out in one of these. Everyone knows not to mess with the neutral zones."

I slide out my side and shut the door behind me before going over to Colt's side. I trust him enough to know he isn't going to lead me into a random dodgy hut, but I also know enough about this messed up fairy tale world I've been led into, that anything is possible.

"I forgot to mention, we are meeting someone here," he tells me just as we get up to the door.

"Who?" I ask him.

"My sister. She is looking forward to meeting you." He looks down at me and chuckles. "Don't look so panicked."

"You didn't tell me I was meeting your family, dressed like this?" I wave a hand out, gesturing to my outfit.

"This is modest. Most supernaturals don't care for wearing much. You will see," he tells me gently, squeezing my hand.

"I thought that was only a wolf thing, as Nikoli never puts clothes on," I say without thinking, but Colt doesn't respond to it. Instead, he leads me through the doorway, and a feeling like someone poured a bucket of water over my head happens. When I open my eyes, water is the first thing I see. Lots and lots of water, and nearly naked people. The middle of the club is a floor composed of three rocks, with a waterfall in the middle, and it's surrounded by glass. There are rock tables, with glass seats, and I can see two bars in the room as well as the floors above and below us. I have to stop looking around to stare at the people in the room; the supernaturals. Colt was right, they do not like clothes. Most of them are wearing the bare minimum to cover themselves. There are so many scents in the room that it's overwhelming, and the noise from the dance music playing is loud, but not loud enough that I need to shout.

"This place is amazing," I say to Colt, who pulls me closer to his side.

"It's your life now. I can show you everything I couldn't before," he tells me, and gently kisses my cheek. I turn my head, both of us staring down at each other. Everything seems to pause as Colt leans forward and presses his lips to mine. He moves his lips slowly, gently, but the passion behind the kiss can't be missed as I copy what he does. If someone told me a year ago, when I met Colt, that I would be kissing him in a supernatural nightclub now, I would have laughed.

"Hey bro, maybe you should put your mate down so I can say hello?" a woman says, and Colt breaks away from the kiss, looking at me for second and turns to look at her. I turn as well, seeing the stunning blonde woman in front of me. This must be his sister. She has blonde hair that is so long it hits the back of her knees, and she has on a very short, pale pink dress. She has long eyelashes, expressive lips, and bright purple eyes that watch me. She looks a lot like Colton; they have the same eyes, the same colour hair, and the same shaped nose.

"Belle, this is Harper. Harper, this is my sister, Belle," Colton introduces us, and she holds a perfectly manicured hand out for me. I step forward and slide my hand into hers.

"So, you're the stupid one that got bit by a wolf, when you're destined for a vampire," she laughs, holding my hand tight enough to hurt me. I squeeze her hand as tight as I can as I take another step closer.

"I'm destined for not just a vampire, Belle," I say, and she laughs.

"I like you, you don't back down, but I could use my hand back," she says, and I drop her hand as Colt slides his hand around my waist.

"Be nice, Belle," he warns her.

"Okay, baby brother. I guess I can be nice to your little wolf," she chuckles. "I'm going to dance. Talk soon." She winks at us and then walks down the steps, and around the waterfall to the bottom level.

"Let's get some drinks," Colt says and leads me to the waterfall, where one of the bars sits on the other side. Colt orders us some drinks, keeping an arm around me the whole time, like he expects me to run off. We find some seats near the waterfall, with Colt at my side, and I pick up the purple drink he got me.

"What is it?" I ask him.

"Drink and see," he chuckles. I place the cocktail to my lips and take a sip. It tastes of blueberries, my favourite. I look in shock at the glass, which refills itself as I watch.

"Fey magic. A never-ending drink." He chuckles at my shocked face, and drinks his own dark blue drink.

"I don't think your sister liked me," I say, and he shakes his head.

"It's not that she doesn't like you. She doesn't trust you with me. She knows we aren't mated, and you're living with wolves. Belle is just protective of me."

"I don't live with them to upset you, or because I don't want to be with you, Colt," I tell him, taking another sip of my drink.

"I know you don't. I know you need time, and I would wait forever. But it's difficult not being able to see you every day, like I was used to doing. I miss you," he tells me, and I lean my head on his shoulder.

"I miss you too. I don't want to be away from you so much, but I don't see how Nikoli would let you come and move in with the pack," I say. I know that wouldn't happen, but I guess I really never thought of the long-term problems we are going to end up having. If I'm split between them permanently, I'm always going to be leaving one to go to the other.

"I wouldn't move without my family either," he says gently, and I sigh.

"This is impossible. Why were we fated to all be together, when it clearly just can't work?" I say, sitting back on my seat and looking at my drink like it holds all the answers in the world.

"Let's not worry tonight. Let's just drink and forget all the serious stuff for a night. We are too young to be worrying about everything all the time," he tells me, and I grin up at him, leaning up and kissing him gently.

"I like that idea," I whisper against his lips that turn up in a smirk as I lean back and down my drink.

"Come and dance with me," he whispers back, drinking more from his glass, and offering me a hand to help me off my seat. We walk hand in hand down the rock steps to the lower floor, which is just a dance floor full of dancing people. I don't have long to look around. As the music gets louder, the further we walk into the crowds of people, and Colt pulls me to his chest. He sways with me, one hand on my hip and the other at the back of my neck. I rest my head on his chest, loving the way he moves our bodies. At least one of us knows what we are doing.

"I could do this all night," he whispers to me, before gently kissing the top my ear. I look up at him, and he kisses my lips deeply.

"Me too," I whisper against his lips. And I mean every word.

CHAPTER SEVENTEEN
NIKOLI

"That's it. I'm going out to look for her. She has been gone for hours, and I know that damn vampire has taken her out," I say, storming out of the kitchen and reaching the front door as it's opened. Colton practically falls through the door, holding Harper up, his arm around her back, and the smell of fey alcohol fills the room. Harper has on a short black dress, looking beyond sexy and so relaxed that I don't have it in me to lecture her about how worried I was. I forget she is only eighteen, and as much as I hate the bastard for taking her out, she might have needed that escape from everything. I just hope she wasn't running from me. It takes a lot of work to swallow the part of me that wants to pick the vampire up and throw him across the driveway.

"Nicky," Harper says in a blurry voice and then laughs when she tries to stand up straight and wave at me.

"Seems she is okay," Gold says, coming out the kitchen. "Other than out of her face on fey drinks." She laughs at the sight of my drunk destined mate and the drunk vampire at her side.

"Wait, I know you're mad at me, but-" she goes to say as she steps forward, but then trips. Colton catches her, just about.

"Let's just get her up to bed," I groan, walking over and lifting Harper into my arms. I'm surprised that Colton doesn't try to stop me, but I do hear him following Gold and me up the stairs. I carry her to her room, laying her on the bed, and Colton pulls a blanket over her.

"Don't kill each other, boys, because if you did, neither of you would get her in the end. She doesn't know it, but she likes, even loves, you both," Gold tells us from the doorway and then walks out. I stare at Colton as he looks down at Harper and despite hating the man for being her mate, I know he is in the same situation I am. My mother's words come back to me, how she used to say everything is fated by the gods. That our mates are chosen, that everything in our world happens for a reason. I know Colton wouldn't be here if he didn't love her, if it wasn't meant to be.

"We should talk, before I do something stupid, like throwing you out the window I had to fix," I say, and he laughs as he looks at the fixed window.

"Alright, wolf," he says, and I walk out of the room, with him following. We go downstairs, into my office. I shut the door behind him and pour a glass of vodka from the small bar off to the side. Colton sits down in the chair in front of the desk, and I take the one behind, without a thought of offering him a drink. It's clear he has already had enough.

"I'm going to make this clear. Don't take her out of my pack again"—I hold my hand up when he goes to respond—"without telling me. I don't care if you want to see her, or take her out to relax or whatever, but I was worried. She means everything to me. I just need to know she is safe," I tell him.

"I am sorry about that. I didn't think you would let her out, but it was immature of me not to ask you first. I'm not used to sharing Harper, or having rules to follow with her. Her foster parents never cared where she was. It's not an excuse, but I'm still getting used to her having other people that love her," he says, making my respect for him grow. I want to hate the blond, annoying vampire in front me, but I can't find myself doing so.

"I'm going to be honest; I don't want to share her. Not with you, not with anyone," I say, and he nods with a sad look.

"Neither do I, but I won't lose her. I won't walk away or fight you because that would only hurt her. She likes you; whether or not she has admitted that to herself, I don't know. But I know it would break her to leave you," he tells me, rubbing his face with his hands.

"I don't want to lose her either," I mutter, leaning back in my seat.

"Then what are we going to do?" Colton asks me.

"Learn to share. Learn to get along and try for Harper. I've seen it work in my pack, with more than just two males involved. If they can do it, then we can." It's not perfect, but nothing about the world I live in is. "You know what? Since I met you, my wolf hasn't done anything but be curious about you. Every vampire I've ever met, my wolf goes mad and tries to attack them, but it treated you like part of the pack straightaway. I trust my wolf's judge of character; he is never wrong."

"I can share her with you. Or learn to. I will do anything not to lose her, and I suppose you're not too bad a wolf," he says with a grin, which I find myself returning.

"Right. Well, tell me about your coven. I need to learn about you," I ask him, and he leans back in his seat.

"I'm going to need a drink for a long conversation like this, and somewhere to sleep tonight. I want to see Harper in the morning and make sure she is okay," he says.

That's fair enough. We have plenty of room in the house to find him a place for the night. I guess it's my first sign of trust if I do this, and he tells me about his coven.

"Done," I tell him, and get up to make him a drink.

CHAPTER EIGHTEEN
HARPER

I blink my eyes open, feeling my head banging and a flood of memories of last night coming back to me. The dancing with Colt, the drinks, the kisses. I reach up and touch my dry lips with my fingers. Those kisses are not something I will be forgetting anytime soon. The way we moved our bodies together, how he kissed down my neck in between songs and finally found my lips. I feel like his kisses, and every stroke of his hands, are burned into my memory.

"Morning stops out," Gold says in a loud, happy voice that makes me want to kill her. I look up to see her walking in the room with a cup of tea in her hands and a massive grin. I sit up in bed, the room spinning a little, as she hands me the cup of tea. The tea looks normal but smells horrible, and I raise my eyebrows at Gold as I push the drink away.

"There's wolfsbane in there, it has healing properties for wolves. Might help with the hangover," she tells me. "But it smells and tastes horrible." She pushes the teacup closer to me. I thought this stuff hurt wolves, but I guess that's another rumour from tv shows.

"I guess it's my own fault for drinking," I say as I take a sniff of the drink and mentally try to forget the horrible smell.

"The fey drinks are addictive though, so I get it. I've had many hangovers from them. Whoever invented the drink that just refills itself, is evil. I came to that conclusion ages ago," she says.

"What are fey like?" I ask, actually wondering.

"Pretty and shiny; their skin gleams. I don't know too much about them, they are a private race and like their own company. They live in trees, singing to plants to make them blossom or die, depending on the season."

"That's cool, and they make strong magic drinks," I add in.

"That's what they are most known for; getting teenage wolves drunk," she says and laughs.

"Is Nikoli mad?" I ask quietly, drinking some of the tea and trying not to gag at the awful taste.

"Not mad, exactly, but he just looked upset," she replies gently.

"I feel bad. I should have said something. I was just worried he wouldn't let me go." I remember his worried face when we got back to the pack. I think I might have called him Nicky. Oh God. I so hope that was a dream and didn't really happen.

"He might have, but you need to trust him. Nikoli sees all his pack members as his responsibility, and leaving the pack without another wolf is against the rules. Not all supernaturals are good, and if something went wrong last night, Nikoli would blame himself forever."

"I don't know what to say. I feel horrible," I mumble, knowing she is right, and I should have thought about it like that. I would never want him to feel responsible for me, but I know he does.

"See, I know the problem," she says, and I raise my eyebrows. "You were brought up in foster care and never had a family who worry about you. You have a family now; a massive pack, and we would do anything to keep you safe. Just think about it because Nikoli wasn't the only one that was worried." She stands up, walking towards the door.

"I care about you too, you know? I never had a best friend before," I say.

"Well, you have one now." She winks at me.

"Have a shower and come down to the kitchen for breakfast," she says with a smile, shutting the door behind her. I sit back in the bed and drink the rest of the horrible tasting tea, surprised that I feel much better and my headache is gone. I get into the shower and start washing my hair, thinking about what Gold said.

I guess I never had to worry about people missing me, about them worrying about me. I don't know how to get used to having this amount of people caring, but I know I won't do what I did last night again. I will tell Nikoli when I want to leave with Colton because I can't give him up. I get out the shower, and towel dry my hair, brushing it and leaving it down before getting dressed in jeans and a tank top. I leave my room and run down the stairs, passing Tam on the way, who says hello. I walk down the corridor and stop in my tracks when I hear Colt talking. *What is he doing here?*

"Colt?" I ask, walking into the kitchen and see

him eating breakfast next to Nikoli. The two of them stop talking when they look at me and smile.

"Come and eat," Nikoli says, standing up, offering me the chair next to him. I slide into the chair and keep my eyes on both Nikoli and Colt. I'm sure I look as confused as I feel.

"How are you feeling?" Colt asks me.

"Good. Gold got me some wolfsbane tea, or I think that's what it's called," I say, and he nods.

"Ah yes, I had some this morning from Nik. The stuff tastes horrible, but it works." He taps his head, and I don't know what I'm more in shock about. The fact he is sitting here and has apparently been here all night and morning. Or the fact Nikoli let him call him Nik, and got him a cup of healing tea for his head. *What the hell happened when I was sleeping? Did I wake up in another world?*

"I have to go, but can I have a moment alone with Harper before I leave?" Colt asks Nikoli, who, to my shock, nods and walks out the room, even shutting the door behind him.

"How did you do that?" I ask, waving my hand towards the door Nikoli left through.

"We spoke and decided that we need to attempt getting along to make this work between us all. Neither of us wants to lose you, and everything happens for a reason, so here I am," Colt says, and I sit in silence, completely baffled. Colt moves from his seat and comes over to me, grabbing my knees and turning me in my chair so he can part my legs and step in between them. I gasp when he slides his hand into my hair, pulling me up to meet his lips. This kiss is nothing like the last one, which was gentle. This time, he kisses me like he can't get enough. *And neither can I.* I wrap my arms around his shoulders, moaning a little when he presses his hard-on close to me, and his other hand slides down my back, grabbing my ass and pulling me closer to him.

"On Tuesday, can you stay over at my house?" He pulls away a little, to look at me. I'm too breathless and turned on to do anything other than nod. Colt grins, kissing me lightly this time, before stepping away and walking to the door.

"By the way, I can't wait to see you Tuesday, and I'm missing you already," he says and then walks out, leaving the door open. I hear him talking to Nikoli outside the room, but I can't hear their words. Seconds later, Nikoli walks into the room. He doesn't even look mad, just calm, and I don't know what to say to him.

"Do you want some bacon, eggs, and beans?"

he asks me, going over to the counter where there is food warming on the stove.

"Sure, thank you," I respond, and he dishes me up a plate before bringing it over and placing it in front of me. There's an awkward silence between us for a while as I eat before I blurt out an apology.

"I'm really sorry for last night. It was cruel and childish to sneak out and not tell you where I was. All I can say is that I'm sorry."

"Harper," he sighs and leans over, picking me up from my chair and putting me on his lap. I can't believe he just lifted me like I was nothing. I pause when he kisses my forehead, his lips staying there for a long time, and I don't feel any reason to move.

"Being alpha means I'm connected to all my wolves, and if you ever mate with me, as the alpha female, you will feel them all too. My wolf and I know we have to protect them because they are weaker than us. Because they need us. I was born to be an alpha, to be protective of those I know are mine, and I can't help that side of myself. I don't want to control you, Harper. I just want to know you're safe."

"I'm not used to people, other than Colt, caring about me. Being protective of me," I whisper.

"That's got to change now. You're not human

anymore, and you are certainly not alone. I want you to remember that I'm here, and if you want to go with Colt, please just tell me," he murmurs softly.

"I was worried you would get jealous, and not let me go," I tell him honestly.

"I might have gotten jealous, I might not have understood the vampire before last night, but I trust him with you. I see the way he looks at you, I know he would die to protect you, and that's enough for me to know you're safe with him," he says gently.

"You seemed to have changed your tune," I whisper.

"We spoke a lot last night. He told me about his coven, how he doesn't drink from humans or hunt them. How his coven is the same. I know he isn't a bad guy; just young and a little foolish," he chuckles. "But for someone his age, he isn't a complete fool,"

"We're the same age," I chuckle.

"I know, and I know you need someone like him around; someone you can relax with, and that can't be me," he says.

"You make it sound like you offer me nothing, Nikoli, when that's not true."

"I know. We just need to get to know each other better."

"First off, did you cook this?" I ask, and he nods.

"It's amazing. Could you teach me how to cook? None of my foster parents would let me near the kitchens; they thought I would steal too much food or something. Who knows?" I say, and shrug my shoulders.

"How about we make some cupcakes? They are nice and easy to make," he says with a smile when I nod, and kisses the side of my head before standing us both up. "Okay, you get the flour, sugar, and eggs out of the cupboards. I will find the rest."

I search the cupboards for the things we need, placing them on the side. Nikoli puts butter, two bowls, and an electric mixer on the side next to us. I watch as he gets out a scale and we measure all the ingredients to match the weight of the two eggs. After we have weighed them all, we put them all in a bowl and Nikoli shows me how to turn the whisk on. It takes a few minutes to mix everything together.

"Okay, try some," he says, putting his finger in the mixture and lifting it into his mouth. I catch his hand, pulling his finger close to my lips, and suck

"So, let's eat and drink," Nikoli thunders, his voice carrying around the room, and someone cues some light music. I settle into my seat and start putting food on my plate; it's all fantastic and well-cooked.

"So, we are going to town tomorrow to get some clothes and other bits. Would you like to come?" Snow asks me.

"I would love to," I reply, and she nods, going back to cutting up Arisa's food for her.

"I'm coming too." Gold adds.

"I have to leave next week; the prince has a job for me," Erik states, and Snow glares at him over Arisa's head.

"I want you to stay for the next month, Erik. With me having a new mate, I want you to help out with the pack," Nikoli says. His words are demanding, and it's apparent when Erik looks over at Nikoli, that he isn't impressed.

"Fine," he says, and pushes his chair out before storming out the room. I glance over at Snow, who just looks down at her plate, sadness written all over her face.

"Mummy, why is Daddy angry all the time?" Arisa asks.

"Because he just is, Arisa. Maybe one day, he will be happier," Snow replies.

"Can't you make him happy, Mummy? My teacher said that destined wolves make each other happy."

"Your teacher is right most the time, Arisa, but not this time. Now, eat your food," Snow says gently, and she nods, turning her attention to her plate. There's a tense silence until Snow smiles over at me before she speaks.

"So, did you have any plans before the rogue?"

"Like job-wise?" I ask.

"Yes, or travelling. Anything, really."

"Well, I like to paint, but I didn't see myself getting a good job out of that. Colton used to collect the paintings I did in school. He said I was good too," I tell her.

"You should practise and then maybe you could get a job selling paintings," she says, and I shake my head. I'm really not that good.

"I have something to show you after you're finished," Nikoli comments, and I nod, going back to eating my food. After dessert, me and Nikoli help carry the empty plates to the kitchens, before helping them clear away some of the food.

"Go, I've got this." Gold waves me away when I

try to help her wash up, and points at Nikoli, who is waiting by the door. I give her a thankful look and walk over to him, sliding my hand into his.

"So, what did you want to show me?"

"A room," he says mysteriously. I laugh and let him lead me up the two flights of stairs to our floor, and instead of going into any of our rooms, he opens the third door I haven't seen used. Nikoli turns the lights on as he walks in and I shut the door behind us. I turn around just in time to see him pull a white sheet off a large easel. It's an old-fashioned wooden one, which is massive and placed right in front of the window. The rest of the room has white sheets covering things, and I wait as Nikoli opens the blinds that cover the window.

"This was my father's study; he used to paint. What you said at dinner; well, I thought you might like to use it," he says softly, and then goes around the room, pulling the white sheets down that are covered in dust. There is a mixture of everything in here, and half-finished canvas paintings of wolves on the wall.

"I will ask Snow and Gold to take you to a paint shop and get you whatever you need," he tells me.

"I'm not that good, and I don't want you to give me this, and waste money on me," I say quietly, and he walks over to me, placing his finger under my chin and lifting my face, so I have to look up into his eyes.

"Doesn't matter to me. Please just consider this a gift."

"And you don't want anything in return?" I ask quietly, and he smirks at me.

"Well, there is one thing."

"What?" I ask, laughing a little when he suggestively wags his eyebrows.

"I want you to paint something for me," he says, and I step forward, placing my hands on his chest. I look up at him as he wraps his arms around me.

"Okay," I reply simply, before resting my head on his chest, and we hold each other for a long time. I don't know what changed between us, but something did, and I like it.

CHAPTER TWENTY

HARPER

"**T**hat looks great on you. Red is really your colour," Gold says, as I smooth down the red jumper and look in the changing room mirror. The red does suit my brown hair and pale complexion. As I see in the mirror more, I find it so strange to think how different I am, now I'm a wolf, but don't look any different. I expected to have flawless skin and big boobs or something, but nope, I still look the same. *It's never like the books.*

"I feel bad spending Nikoli's money to get these clothes. I have to get a job or something to repay him," I say, knowing I can't rely on him; but then, I have so little clothes that are suitable for the cold weather.

Snow and Gold also took me to an art shop earlier that was a little out of the central part of town, and helped me pick out paints and brushes that I would need. We picked out a few different sized canvas and other bits.

"He wouldn't want you to. Not yet, as your wolf is too new, and you could shift if you feel threatened. Give it a few months, and maybe you could look into the local university jobs. Or jobs with the pack? Or maybe your vampire coven has jobs?" she offers, and I nod, wondering how threatened I'd have to feel to let my wolf take over.

I feel like I can trust her, now that she is a part of me; a piece that I felt like I was always missing. I grew up so alone, and it's strange to always have my wolf with me, so I'm never alone again. As painful as it was to get bitten by that rogue, in a way, I'm thankful that he did bite me because I got my wolf from that.

I pull the jumper off and add it to the ever-growing pile of clothes in the basket. I pull my black jumper back on, and Snow uses Nikoli's card to pay for the clothes before we leave. Snow explained how the pack all share money and get a lot from the investment shares their parents left them, so money isn't an issue. But I still intend to pay him back for all this somehow.

"We could go to the local chip shop on the way home and get some food. Nikoli loves the fish they do there," Snow tells me, and I give her a little smile as we walk from the shops to the car park across the street.

I press the lift button as Gold says, "Shoot, I forgot to pay for the ticket. I'll be right back," and she walks off. I follow Snow into the elevator, and she presses the button to go to our level.

"Have you spoken to Nikoli much?" she asks me.

I woke up this morning after our Sunday pack meal, and I will admit that I looked around for him, but couldn't find him. By the time I made breakfast and ate with Gold, Snow came in and said we were going shopping. I know I'm going to formally meet Colton's parents tomorrow, and then spending the night with his coven, so I wanted to spend the day with Nikoli.

"No, why?"

"It's painful for a male mate to be around his female, and not act on it. I thought you should know, as I know he wouldn't tell you. It would be the same for Colton. A lot of people are shocked that he managed to spend a year with you, and not make a move," she tells me softly.

The thought of Nikoli or Colton being in any kind of pain makes me feel horrible. I didn't know that it would do that to them. I thought we had enough time to get to know each other more, and make the lifelong decision later on. It's not like I'm not attracted to them both because I am; far more than I've been drawn to anyone in my life.

"Hey, little wolves," a deep voice greets us as the lift doors open, and three large men stand in a line outside. All of them are overweight, with large stomachs and round faces. They look around forty, and I would guess they are related to each other, from the same wiry blond hair they have. One of the men steps forward, his dark eyes locking with mine.

"We have come to claim the new wolf; her. She is my mate," he says, pointing at me. He lets out a long laugh as Snow steps forward, dropping the bags in the doorway of the lift, to keep it from closing.

"How did you come to that conclusion?" she muses, cocking her head to the side. I know he isn't my mate or anyone I would ever be with. The lust-filled look in his eyes is creeping me out, and no part of my wolf is making me want to go to him, like it does when I'm around Nikoli or Colton.

"I smelt her, and I know," he says, still watching me.

"I'm not your mate," I say to him, and he laughs, just as Snow shifts suddenly into a giant white wolf, her clothes ripping to pieces on the floor around her. *I know why she is called Snow now.* Snow lets out a loud growl as she crouches down, and I turn slightly when I hear Gold's heels clicking across the car park. She walks over from the stairs and stops right next to us.

"Now, now. If you believe Harper is your mate, then issue a formal challenge to our alpha, as he has claimed her as his. As I'm sure you already know," she says.

"On the next full moon, we will attack your pack. We will take back our lands; our people and my mate will kneel for me," the man says, and I find myself growling as my wolf pushes against my mind. Her only thought is attacking him and getting rid of the problem, and I have to force her to stop when I see my arm starting to grow fur. It's a real fight, and I end up closing my eyes, hardly hearing Gold as she speaks.

"It's not smart to tell your enemies when you're going to attack, boys… but the challenge is accepted. I speak as one of the betas of the Forest pack," Gold says, placing her hand on my arm. The simple touch seems to reassure my wolf, as she stops pushing. I open my eyes to see the three men step away slowly.

"I will never mate with you. I would die first," I say, a growl slipping out my throat as I speak, and the man gives me a slightly creepy smile, stopping in his tracks.

"Is that a promise, little wolf? You can run all you like, but I will find you," he says, his voice echoing around the car park.

"Leave before I decide to kill you myself and screw the rules," Gold snaps out, taking a step in front of me, trying to block the man from seeing me, but I still hear him.

"Remember to run, little wolf. Catching you will be fun," he laughs, before turning around and walking away.

"What are they?" I ask Gold when they have left. Snow pushes her head against my hip in a sign of comfort, and I slip my hand into her fur. The man's last words are racing through my mind. *Run, little wolf.*

"Hogs, which are basically massive black pigs. Disgusting shifters they are, and there is no real use for them. Wolves, on the other hand, are natural hunters, and we balance out the countryside. Hogs; well, they can kill you by running into you, but have no real brains to speak of when they shift. They just kill. The only issue is that they have a high reproductive rate, compared to other shifters, so their pack is massive," Gold tells me.

"Why would they say I'm his mate?" I ask, knowing it isn't true. It doesn't feel right.

"They had wanted a reason to attack the pack for a long time because Nikoli killed their last alpha's when he didn't have a choice. He did let them live, and this is how they repay him. Some laws stop them from attacking us now, like their parents attacked Nikoli and Snow's parents years ago. We have a royal family who enforces these laws after so many of our kind was killed. There used to be thousands of breeds, but now there isn't. The only reason a challenge is allowed is that of a mate."

"How long until the next full moon?" I ask, dreading the answer.

"Ten days, Harper. We need to go and tell Nikoli. We need to plan, and our pack won't be strong enough to win this alone," Gold says, picking up the bags.

I hear a woman scream before I can think about her words. I look over to see a middle-aged woman watching us – well, more looking at Snow – with evident fear, as she comes out of the stairwell.

"It's okay. This is my dog, and she escaped my car. I've been looking everywhere for her," I say, stroking Snow's head. The woman nods, not moving, as she plants herself as close to the door as possible.

"Come on, Little Snow, time to go back home," I say, and Gold chuckles as we walk away.

"Little Snow? Are you kidding; she is a huge white wolf!"

"I couldn't say Big Snow; it just sounds strange, and would have freaked her out more," I laugh back. The humour of the situation slips away as I realise how much danger we are in now, and the Hog's words move around my mind one more time.

Run, little wolf.

CHAPTER TWENTY-ONE
HARPER

"What's wrong?" Nikoli asks as we all walk into the gym, his eyes meeting mine. I don't know how he can tell something is wrong, but he does. I watch as he drops the weights he was lifting and runs over to us. The gym has five men in it that I haven't seen before, and they all go silent as they watch us.

"The Hogs have claimed that Harper is their mate. They declared that they are going to attack us at the next full moon," Gold says, and a ripple of anger flows over Nikoli's face as he steps closer and puts his hands on both my arms.

"Are you okay?" he asks. "If they hurt you, screw the rules, I'm going to kill them all."

I can sense how worried he is without listening to his threatening words; the slight growling I hear only confirms what I can detect. I move closer and wrap my arms around him, laying my head on his chest.

"I'm fine. They didn't touch me. We just spoke, that's all."

My words seem to have the desired effect, as the light growling stops, and Nikoli wraps his arms around me, kissing the top of my head.

"Then we fight them. They have wanted this since I killed their parents and took back the land they stole. This is personal between us," Nikoli shouts, and I hear growling replies scattered around the room.

"I'm sorry you have to be involved," Nikoli whispers to me.

"I'm here now, and I want to help," I say, making Nikoli tense up a little.

"Gold, call a meeting for the whole pack tonight. Snow, could you find my betas and tell them to go to my office."

"We can't win this alone. Maybe I should call Colton, as his coven is in town and might be willing to fight. The Hogs would never expect vampires," Snow says.

"Fine, call Colton. I will be there soon, but I want a moment alone with Harper," Nikoli says, holding me close the entire time he speaks.

"Sure," Snow says.

I hear everyone leave, but we don't move. I feel safe in his arms, secure, and that's not something I remember feeling growing up. The very thought that someone could take this from me just panics me. I can't lose him, or Colton. Not now; not ever.

"Let me take you somewhere. I want to show you something," he says, and I nod, stepping away and letting him take my hand. I've never had someone this close to me; no one other than Colton. My friend Skye was close to me, but I doubt she will miss me much. We only saw each other once a week after school finished, and I never trusted her like I should have. I never let myself get close to anyone other than Colton; now I have a whole pack. I have Gold and Snow, two women I consider close friends. *And two destined mates, I can't forget about those*. We walk out of the training room and around it, towards the gardens at the side of the house.

"I grew up here; my mother loved these

gardens. She had a thing for *The Secret Garden* fairy tales, and recreated her own one with my father's help. He would have done anything for her," Nikoli tells me as we walk down a stone path, filled with flowers on each side. At the end of the short path is a big vine-covered door.

"This is yours now," Nikoli says, and pulls a necklace out his pocket. There's a medium-sized old-looking key on the end. The necklace is silver and has roses engraved on it, with an 'F' on the handle. I'm sure it stands for the Forest pack.

"I can't accept that," I say, as he presses it into my hand.

"My mother put this around my neck when she made me run from the pack as a child. I will never forget seeing her for the last time as she pushed us into one of the old tunnels in the woods. She crouched down, with tears running down her face, and Snow holding on to my hand. She told me to give it to my mate and to have a future. That, no matter what happens, she wanted me to be happy, and I am with you, Harper. Please, let me fill her wishes," he confesses, making me want to cry for the child he was. That must have been horrible, knowing he couldn't save her, and having to protect himself and his sister instead. Nikoli steps closer as we both stare at each other. The emotion in his eyes is hard to see, but I don't want to look away. I want to be here for him.

"I've worn this for many years, waiting to give it you, Harper," he tells me, forcing me to stare into his bright blue eyes, like he is everything to me as I am to him. Except it isn't just him wanting to be with me anymore; it's me. I want to be with him more now than I ever have. This means a lot to him, and I don't know how to feel about it. I never had anything from my own parents; there was nothing left in the fire, apparently.

"Are you sure?" I ask him gently.

"I've never been more certain of anything in my life," he tells me, making me wonder if he means more than just the key. I close my hand around it and walk towards the door, feeling him watching me. The key is hard to turn, as it's so small for the large door, but I finally manage and push the door open with my shoulder. The garden is impressive, just like the secret garden in the fairy tale, complete with a swing in the middle of it. I don't know where to look, there is just so much colour in the garden; it's so alive. There's an arch in the corner, and I put the necklace on before walking over to it, with Nikoli following me. The arch has dozens of roses around it, and I go to touch one, pricking my finger on a thorn.

"Ouch," I say, pulling my hand away. Nikoli takes my hand in his, putting my finger in his mouth as I watch in shock. What feels like years later, but it must have only been seconds, he lets go, and I look at my finger in shock. *There's no cut anymore.*

"It's strange to get used to, the whole healing thing. Everything is hard to get used to. I don't know how to imagine never ageing and being immortal," I say, and he steps closer, pulling me into his arms.

"Immortal life isn't easy, but you have the pack and me. You have Colton and his coven. You won't be alone."

"Do you mean that?" I ask him gently, not trusting my voice. I don't want to let them down.

"Harper," Nikoli says my name slowly, as he pulls me closer. I look up, not moving, as he lowers his head. The first brush of his lips across mine is sweet, tender almost, and then he slides his hand into my hair, kissing me like a starving man. His lips battle against my own, almost punishing me, but in the most seductive way. I can't seem to get enough of how he tastes, or how good his hard body feels pressed against my own. Nikoli pulls away, breathless as I am, and runs his finger across my bottom lip.

"Whatever happens in our future, I'm fighting for you. I'm here for you, and even if you decide not to mate with me, I will be at your side as your friend, as anything I can be for you," he declares, looking into my eyes as he speaks, then letting me go and walking out of the garden as I watch him leave. I want to call him back, to tell him that I want him as much as he apparently wants me, but something stops me. I guess it's a worry of everything being so new and I'm in a world I don't understand. I know I like him, and I want another kiss, but something stops me from running after him. The same part that thinks of Colton.

CHAPTER TWENTY-TWO
COLTON

"W here is she?" I ask as I burst into Nikoli's office, after Snow called me and told me what had happened. I don't pause as I push past the giant wolf and take another step closer. I get that they think I'm a threat to their alpha or whatever, but Harper has been threatened, and I won't have that. No one threatens my Harper.

"Don't," I warn him, and he moves out the way. I reach Nikoli, who is leaning over a map of the house, the forest, and the town. The pack lands actually surround the town; I learned that when I researched everything I could about this pack before I came for Harper.

"Harper is fine, don't worry. I would be out there killing them now if they'd touched her," Nikoli says, and I take a deep breath. As much as I trusted his sister when she told me Harper was okay, I still needed to hear it from her or Nikoli. The rest of the wolves in the room seem to relax at Nikoli's words, not seeing me as such a threat anymore.

"What's the plan?" I ask him, and he nods, looking back at the map. The big guy from before comes over and stands next to me. On the other side of the table is Gold, Harper's friend, and a blond guy I would guess is her brother. The guy who tried to stop me, with dark hair and darker eyes, stands next to Gold.

"Everyone, this is Colton. As you know, he is Harper's other destined mate, and I trust him to help us. We will need this help as we cannot call other packs in to help us. The rules say nothing about covens, or other beings helping us because they wouldn't expect them to help wolves over a mate dispute," Nikoli says, and there's whispered agreements in the room.

"They wouldn't expect vampires; plus, they

move so fast at night, they could kill a lot of them quickly with some weapons," Gold's brother says.

"Who are you?" I ask him, but it's Nikoli who answers.

"That's Erik, and his sister, Gold." He then points at the guy next to me. "This is Lewis. These three are my betas."

"I'm Tam, the pack healer," the other guy next to Gold introduces and I nod.

"Can you help us? From what you have told me, you have a small coven," Nikoli says, and I nod.

"I have family, distant, but they would come here to fight for my mate," I say, after thinking about it for a moment. My mother's sister was turned, and they had many kids, who mated and have their own children now. I know they would come and fight for me, as we stick together. The only reason we aren't in a coven together is that they are old school vampires, and still hunt humans.

"How many?" Nikoli asks me.

"Twenty vampires. The rest live too far away and wouldn't be able to get here in time," I tell them.

"Okay, but make it clear that they can't hunt the humans in town."

"Understood," I reply.

"Right. The best thing we can do is set up a constant patrol until the fight. Groups of five, and they change every two hours," Nikoli says.

"I can sort that," Gold says, pulling out her phone. "I will make a pack group chat, so I can tell everyone when it's their time." *That's smart.*

"Tam, I need you to get the hall ready for the people that cannot fight. Mainly the children. Make sure that every one of the children know where the escape tunnel is, and where it leads. If anything goes wrong, they can escape while I'm sure their parents will fight for them," Nikoli says, and Tam gives him a nod before walking out. "Lewis, you're in charge of weapons and making sure everyone is sorted out."

"I will sort everything, alpha," Lewis responds.

"We have our own weapons," I tell Lewis, who smiles.

"Good vampire," he says and walks out. A man of little words right there.

"How's the group chat going?" I ask Gold.

"Adding seventy people is hard," Gold says, making us all chuckle.

"Erik, I want you to sort out traps. Traps like you make for catching rogues," Nikoli tells him.

"What kind of traps?" I ask, wondering what he could do.

"Pits of silver daggers, basic Hog traps made with silver. Rope catches, that hang the Hogs in the air. Lots of different ones," Erik says, sounding bored, as he waves a hand.

"It would work, slow them down," I comment.

"That it will become, Vampire," he says in a cocky tone. I have no doubt he meant that as an insult.

"It's Colton, not vampire, *wolf*," I say, leaning forward on the table as he growls.

"Enough! Out now, Erik," Gold says, grabbing Erik's shirt and dragging him out the room.

"I'm going to need to move my coven here. It's not going to be safe in the house we are renting for long," I tell Nikoli, who rubs his face with his hand as he leans back in the seat.

"You have a child with you, right?" he asks, referring to my little sister I told him about the other night.

"Yes," I reply.

"Okay, have them come here. There is plenty of room in the house, but they must not feed on anyone here," he warns. "I won't be able to save them or side with your coven if they do."

"We don't feed on humans, let alone wolves," I remind him.

"I believe you or I wouldn't let you come in here," Nikoli tells me.

"Where is Harper? I need to tell her she can't stay on Tuesday. And I just need to see for myself that she is okay."

"I don't know. Maybe she is painting? The room next to her bedroom," he tells me.

"Thanks," I say and walk out as he goes back to looking at his map. I pass a few wolves as I make my way to the stairs and run up the two flights before seeing Harper straightaway. Nikoli was right; she is painting with the door open. I think back to the ten paintings I have in my room that she painted. I love seeing them, they are beautiful, and I know no matter how long I live, they always will be, much like Harper herself. I walk over, leaning against the door, and watching as she moves the brush across the canvas. The painting is just outlined so far, but I think it's the forest, which you can see out the window. It's a beautiful view, and I know her painting will be amazing.

"Are you going to stare all day, or say hello?" she asks, never stopping her movements with the paintbrush. I smile as I walk in the room, closing the door behind me.

"Can't I stare at you? You're beautiful," I comment, and she chuckles as she puts down the brush and looks over her shoulder at me. Harper's hair is up in a messy bun, bits hanging out, and a white coverall over her leggings and top. She has a little white paint smudged on her cheek, and she looks stressed.

"I'm moving in, me and my coven," I tell her, and her big eyes widen.

"Nikoli was okay with that?" she asks.

"Yes. He knows it's the safest thing to do for my coven, and we are going to help win this war. I won't let anyone take you," I tell her, stepping closer and picking her up off the chair.

"I'm scared. Not for myself but for everyone else. I finally have people I care about, and I can't imagine losing even one of them," she whispers, our faces close together.

"I know, but think of it this way; they feel the same about you. They couldn't stomach the thought of losing you, Harper. So, we will all fight for you," I tell her, and she leans forward, gently kissing me.

"I know you're right, but I also don't know how to cope with the idea of losing anyone."

"I will try my hardest to make sure you don't lose anyone," I tell her, and she rests her head on my shoulder as she cries silent tears. She doesn't have to tell me what she is thinking, or say anything. I just hold her as close as I can and be there for her.

CHAPTER TWENTY-THREE
HARPER

"You look so nervous. I'm trying not to laugh," Gold says, and I glare at her as I smooth my red jumper down, then fix my hair for the tenth time. I've changed my clothes four times, and I still don't think I'm looking the best I can. I know it likely doesn't matter what I look like, but I'm still incredibly nervous to meet them.

"I'm meeting Colton's family, his sister was scary as hell, and his parents blanked me the last time we met," I say.

"I thought you said she looked like a Barbie?"

Nikoli says from next to me, his hand tightening in mine.

"A Barbie that transforms into a tiger with sharp claws, perhaps," I mutter, making Gold and Nikoli laugh, and I turn back to look at the front door. I've been waiting here with Gold and Nikoli for the last ten minutes, ever since Colton called to say they were driving here. The front door is knocked on three times before Colton opens the door and walks in, a small girl holding his hand. She is so pretty, with long straight blonde hair, big purple eyes, and a strange blue mark in the middle of her forehead. I can't see what it is from where I'm standing. Colton moves to the side with the girl, and his parents walk in. There's a certain commanding presence to them that you can't help but notice straightaway that they are image of Colt, just older. Both of them are in their forties, or they were turned then, with blond hair, and they have smart clothes on.

"This is my mother, Nita, and my father, Trevor," Colton introduces.

"Don't forget me, I'm here too," the little girl says, and Colton chuckles.

"Everyone, this is Light," Colton introduces her, just as Belle comes through the door with two large pink glitter suitcases, which she rolls straight into the room and drops on the floor between us. She has fewer clothes on than the last time I saw her, if that's even possible. This time, it's pink hot pants and a white lace crop top, with a bright pink bra underneath that you can't miss. I look up to see Nikoli give me a wide-eyed look. Thank God he isn't looking; I'd have to kick him.

"I get the Barbie comment now. She looks exactly like one," Gold says.

"Want to say that again? Maybe closer, wolf?" Belle replies, and Gold shrugs her shoulders as she starts to step forward, but Colton walks in front of his sister.

"We aren't here to fight our allies, remember? What happened in your past is yours to deal with, Belle. These wolves haven't done anything to you," he tells her quietly, and I hear her huff in reply, but she doesn't say a word.

"I saw you in the house, the old house, but Mum and Dad said I couldn't talk to you because you're human," Light tells me, her bright purple eyes staring up at me. She is stunning, even so young. I bet she will break a lot of hearts when she is older.

"Oh, I never knew you were there at all," I tell her.

"I couldn't tell you, in case you wanted to meet her. She is star marked, and you would have asked what the mark was. Plus, she isn't very good at hiding her gifts," Colton explains, and it makes sense.

"Star marked?" I ask.

"When some children are born, they have that mark. These people are usually compelling," Nikoli answers me, staring at the child. "Although I've never actually seen a child like you before," he tells her, and she smiles.

"I can make light," she says and holds out her hands, which start lighting up, so bright that I have to look away.

"Maybe we shouldn't blind our new roommates, Light," Colton's mother says, coming over. She places her hand on Light's shoulder and the light instantly disappears.

"Okay, Mum," Light says, looking up at her with a grin.

"Who are you?" I hear Arisa say, as she runs into the entrance hall and stops to stare at Light. The two of them are really close in age, and I don't think there are many girls Arisa's age around the pack.

"I'm Light, and you're Arisa, the princess. I saw

you in some gardens, much older, with long hair," Light says, and everyone goes silent.

"We think Light has some precognitive powers," Colton fills us in.

"I'm not a princess, just a wolf," Arisa laughs.

"Arisa, why don't you show Light around, that would be lovely," Gold suggests and Arisa nods, holding her hand out for Light. Light runs over and grabs her hand, and I watch as they scamper off.

"I will keep an eye on them," Erik says, and walks off after the girls.

"Making friends her own age would be good for her. She spends all her time learning to control her powers and hanging out with us. She doesn't go to school," Nita tells us.

"We have a school here for our young. She would be welcome to join. I'm sure the teacher could work with you to learn where she is and catch her up. When our children turn twelve, they go to the human school. Two of our wolves are teachers, so they keep an eye on them for us. We feel it teaches them skills about humans and how to interact with them. We don't hide our children away, and we teach them to fight from age thirteen," Nikoli says.

"That would be deeply appreciated, and I agree

with your ideas. I always worried about sending her to school when I cannot keep an eye on her. I can use human makeup to cover her star mark when she goes," Nita says, admiration in her eyes. Nita turns to me, looking me up and down.

"It is lovely to see you again, Harper, though maybe not under these circumstances," Nita says and offers me her hand. I shake it as Trevor comes over to stand next to his wife.

"Nice to see you too," I say to them both.

"I hope you can forget our shortness towards you when you used to come over; we do not like hiding our lives from humans," Trevor says. He still comes across as cold, but I think that's just how he is.

"I understand," I reply.

"Right, awkward family meeting out the way. Why don't we get settled in?" Colton says, stepping closer to me. He pulls me away from Nikoli and into his arms.

"I can show you to your rooms, if you want?" Gold asks.

"Perfect, come on," Nita says, and walks up the stairs, following Gold. Trevor nods at me, and Belle only grins as she walks up the stairs.

"Let's get some food, I'm starving," Colt whispers to me. "Coming, Nik?" Colt watches him as he looks at me for a second.

"We made cupcakes. Well, Harper mainly did. We could eat those," Nikoli says, and I laugh.

"That's not nice, Nikoli," I tell him and look up at Colton. "I burnt them as we kind of got distracted, and forgot they were in the oven," I admit.

"How about we all make some new ones, and not burn them?" Colt laughs.

"Sounds good. I could eat," Nikoli says, and pats his stomach before turning and walking towards the kitchen. I'm honestly surprised that the two men I care the most about in the world actually get along now, and I would even call them friends. Whether they would admit that to each other or not is another matter.

CHAPTER TWENTY-FOUR
NIKOLI

"Still not mated? Man, it's taking you a long time compared to others. Do you need tips on how to flirt?" Erik teases as he sits on my desk. I give him a look that suggests he shuts it.

"It's different for humans, and she was only human last week," I tell him. Despite being my brother-in-law, we are right friends, but I wish he would sort out his relationship with my sister. He will end up losing her, and despite trying to give him advice, I can't make him sort his life out like he really needs to.

"Maybe you should take her out on a date?" he suggests.

"With five days left before the Hogs attack? Or the new vampire coven that has moved into the pack, when most here have no experience with vampires. I'm spending all my time reassuring everyone that they don't eat wolves or hunt humans," I tell him sarcastically, and he nods.

"Don't get grouchy with me brother, I get it. Being near your mate and not mating makes you angry," he tells me, and I manage to make my wolf relax a little, which is getting harder to do. Difficult is an understatement of a word to describe being around my destined mate for so long without mating. Seeing Harper every morning at breakfast and around the pack is difficult; sleeping in the room next to her and not being able to touch her is torture. But I refuse to push her into a massive situation like this, just because we are pressed for time. I want to go into the fight with her at my side as my mate, but I can do it anyway for her. My wolf presses against my mind, imagining how sweet Harper smells and how beautiful she is, both in her human and wolf form.

"I don't want to push her. I already kissed her a

few times, and I'm waiting for her to come to me," I tell him, and he laughs.

"You're so tense and going into a fight not mated, isn't safe. We don't want to lose our alpha because his destined mate is waiting," he tells me, and I give him another look. We aren't meant to be talking about my mating or lack of; we are discussing where we are hiding wolves in the forest for when the Hogs attack. Erik is going to lead a pack of our best fighters, that we are going to hide in the woods, to attack them from behind. I will lead the rest of the wolves into a head-on attack, with Colton and his vampires hiding in the trees as the surprise.

"That's not your issue," I tell him firmly. The door opens, and Harper walks in.

"No, it's mine," she says, apparently hearing our conversation. She looks almost nervous as she watches me. I can't help but take in her tight jeans, little cami top, and cardigan. Her long hair is down, and shapes her beautiful face.

"Leave us, Erik," I tell him, and he nods, sliding off the desk.

"They are going to come here and kill our people. The people you want to fight for you and the man who wants to be your mate. If you feel nothing for him, walk away. If you care at all about this pack, and us, mating is an option you need to think about. The same for your vampire; it's a wonder he hasn't lost his mind yet," he tells her. I go to interrupt him, but Harper holds a hand up to stop me, wanting to hear him out.

"Like how you treat Snow? Wouldn't you regret it if you go into the fight without speaking to her?"

"You have no right to speak to me about my relationship with Snow," Erik snaps.

"Neither do you, about my relationship with Nikoli or Colton. But even if they aren't my mates yet, I still wouldn't ever treat them the way you treat Snow. Don't you think she is hurting too? That she needs you?" she asks, and he steps forward, his head bowed down.

"I just can't. She reminds me-" he starts to say and then stops, storming out the room.

"Should I have not said anything?" Harper says into the silence of the room, looking at the closed door.

"You're an alpha female, and your wolf is protective of the females in the pack. It's normal, and he is mistreating my sister," I tell her. She nods before shutting the door and looking over at me.

"I like you," she says softly, when neither of us

has said anything for a while. I smile, getting up from my desk chair, and walk over to her. When I'm close, I pull her into my arms, loving how she feels against me.

"I don't want you to mate with me because you feel pressured or for any other reason than the most important one," I tell her honestly.

"Which is?" she asks.

"That you love me. That you want to spend forever with me, Harper. I don't want to scare you by telling you how I feel, and what I want." I whisper the last part.

"I just feel like I need to spend more time with you. Get to know you more, but I feel like there's no way to do that with the little time we have," she tells me, and I nod, kissing the top of her head.

"Okay... I have an idea. Come on," I say, sliding my hand into hers and walking her over to the desk. I motion for her to sit in the chair, and then perch on the desk near her.

"I ask one question, you answer, and then you can ask me one," I offer, and she smiles, leaning back in the chair.

"Okay, but I go first," she says, with a slight challenge in her tone.

"Fine," I reply, watching as she crosses her legs and looks me up and down.

"How old are you?" she asks, and I groan, hoping to avoid this one.

"Two hundred and thirty-eight," I say, and she laughs.

"So, I'm crushing on an old man," she says through laughs. I'm not that old compared to some of the wolves I know.

"Do I look like an old man to you?" I say, spreading my arms wide.

"Nope…you certainly do not," she replies.

"My turn. How many guys have you dated?" I ask her, and she blushes slightly before answering.

"Two guys, and to answer your unsaid question, I'm a virgin," she says.

"I never asked," I smirk, trying to keep the happiness out of my face that I'm going to be the first and only one to touch her like that. Well, if she doesn't mate with Colton first, that is. I don't know what her plan is, or if she even has one. I also have no idea how I could share her for our mating.

"My turn." She glares when she sees my big smile.

"How many women have you dated?" she asks,

and I pull on the collar of my shirt a little before answering.

"A few, but none long-term, and no wolves," I tell her, and she keeps eye contact with me for a while before nodding. I always felt sleeping with wolves was disrespectful to my future mate, and it would be weird to live with them around after. Not that I dated much; work has always been more important.

"If you could travel anywhere on holiday, where would you go?" she asks.

"To New York. I've always wanted to see the city that never sleeps. To try some of the unusual foods I've heard they have," I reply. Running a pack means I haven't had much time to travel and hopefully when things settle, I can take Harper somewhere.

"I want to go there too, and I know what you mean. I saw something on the news the other day about a cupcake vending machine. It gives you a choice of freshly-made cupcakes, and boxes them up. There is apparently a ten-minute wait to get one," she tells me, and I smile. That's exactly something I would want to take her to.

"Yes, things like that. Maybe we could go there

one day," I say, and she nods, a slight blush tingeing her cheeks.

"My turn," she states, standing up and stepping closer to me. She stops when she is positioned between my open legs. She places her hands on my thighs and looks down.

"If I asked you to kiss me now, would you?" she asks, and I smirk, sliding my hand into her soft hair and leaning up.

"The answer to that is always yes," I tell her, and place my lips on hers.

CHAPTER TWENTY-FIVE
HARPER

"**H**ave you seen Colt or Nikoli?" I ask Tam as I pass his room. I've been looking for either of them all morning, but I can't find them.

"Training," he tells me before giving me a little smile and going back to his paperwork in front of him. I walk down the corridor towards the back of the house, and open the closed doors to the training room. The room keeps the sound in, so when I open the door, I'm met with a big crowd that is cheering. They don't even notice me open the door and I push through the people to get to the front to see what they are cheering for. I stop when I see

Colt and Nikoli, both of them with long silver spears in their hands, and it's clear they have been fighting for a while. I never really thought about how lucky a woman I am, but seeing both my destined mates topless, I realize I'm quite fortunate. They are complete opposites of each other. Colt, with his light blond hair, thinner build, and playful face. Then there is Nikoli. He is built huge, like most shifters, with his dark hair and a serious expression that I rarely see leave his face. However, they are nothing like the saying I've heard; opposites *do not* attract. If anything, they just explode. What I'm sure started as training has changed because they are both hitting each other as hard as they can. Nikoli flips backwards, putting space between him and Colton, and landing perfectly, but Colton uses his ability to move so fast to land a hit on Nikoli's arm as he falls. Nikoli swings his own spear around, and Colton blocks it before it makes contact. Over and over, they place to hit after hit.

"That's the best you have, wolf?" Colton teases, and Nikoli only growls in warning before his strikes become brutal and he lands another strong hit to Colton's back. My wolf growls, and my body starts shaking as I watch them fight with each other. While some part of me knows it's just training, another part of me wonders if this will be what happens if I ever mate with one of them. They would never let me be with them both; this fight alone proves they are nowhere near being friends. My wolf fills my mind, and I let her take over, shifting and feeling people move away from me. My wolf runs straight over to Colt and Nikoli, jumping in the middle of them, and they both instantly stop.

"Harper?" Colt asks, and it dawns on me that he hasn't seen me like this. I look up as he puts the spear gently on the ground and lifts a hand towards me. Anger fills me when I look at the blood pouring down the side of his head; he's hurt.

"Harper, it was just training," Nikoli says to me, but my wolf doesn't want to listen. She turns and runs out the open door on the other side of the room, hearing Colt and Nikoli calling after me, yet ignoring them. As my wolf runs through the house and into the woods, the image of Nikoli and Colt trying to kill each other just races through my mind. They could do that; they would kill each other over me. My wolf whines as she reaches the lake in the middle of the woods and I remember my human form as she crouches down. She lets me shift back, and I sit naked on the stones by the lake. I pull my knees to my chest, watching the calm lake. Tears fall down my face as I try to make everything work in my head. I remain in place, even when I hear two people coming towards me from behind, their feet crunching on the fallen leaves.

"Aren't you cold? Or do wolves not get cold?" Colt asks when I feel him step to the left of me and Nikoli pauses on the other side.

"We feel the cold, but it's never that bad. We won't get ill or die from it," Nikoli answers his question.

"Can we sit?" Colt asks me gently after a few moments of silence. I don't answer, but I nod my head, keeping still as they sit on either side of me. Both of them are pressed close to my sides, keeping me warm.

"What happened today?" Nikoli asks me.

"Seeing you both fight like that, it scared me."

"Because you think we will kill each other, or attempt to kill each other like we fight in training?" Colt says, knowing me well enough to guess.

"Harper. I won't lie to you. The number of times I thought about killing the vampire is high, but you know what changed only recently?" Nikoli asks me gently.

"What?" I whisper.

"He is my friend," Nikoli tells me, and I know he wouldn't lie to me.

"Same here," Colt answers, and I sit quietly as I take in their words. I look over at Nikoli, who keeps eye contact with me and nods once before I look over at Colt. Colt holds a hand out for me, and I take it, letting him help me stand. I hear Nikoli stand up behind me, and there's silence as I realise that I'm naked between them, and they aren't arguing. I lean forward, kissing Colt gently, pulling away before he can even grab me for a deeper kiss. I mentally hold my breath as I turn around and walk up to Nikoli, who tensely keeps his hands at his sides but doesn't stop me as I lean up and kiss him the same way I did Colton.

"This can work?" I ask when I step back, and they both answer in unison.

"Yes."

CHAPTER TWENTY-SIX
HARPER

"Tell me a story, please? I've read all these books, and you must know some kind of story," Arisa begs as I attempt to put her to bed. I turn and smile at Nikoli, who watches me from the door. We had a pack meal today, and it would have been awkward if it wasn't for Arisa, who sat on my lap and helped herself to my food. Snow and Erik said she hadn't stopped speaking about me since we met. When she asked me to put her to bed, I really didn't have a choice. I tuck the sheets closer around her and nod.

"How about *Little Red Riding Hood*, but with a

twist?" I ask her, and she nods happily, cuddling a small little fairy doll.

"So, once upon a time, a young girl had just turned eighteen and went to the forest to celebrate her birthday with her friends. The girl wore a red coat and had long brown hair. After walking into the woods, she saw a wolf, and the silly wolf bit her."

"Oh no," Arisa says, and I nod, holding her hand.

"But it was all for the best, as the girl turned into a wolf herself and then met another wolf. He was a very handsome wolf, who was kind and sweet at times. Before she realised it, she had fallen in love with him," I say, my eyes resting on Nikoli as I speak, and he parts his lips in shock. I've been silly avoiding my feelings for him up to this point; I knew how I felt the moment I met him. Every day we have spent together after that has just confirmed how he is everything I thought he was. No wonder my wolf chose him.

"So, she got her happily ever after?" Arisa asks with a yawn, and I smile, pushing a little bit of her hair off her face.

"Yes, she did. Good night, Arisa." I stand up and walk out the room, letting Nikoli close the door behind me. The second it's closed, he pulls me closer and kisses me. He walks me backwards, until my back hits the wall near the door, as he continues to devour my lips.

"Let's go to your room," I say, breaking away, and he gently kisses me once more.

"Are you sure?" he asks, and I slide my hand into his, leading him towards the stairs to our floor. I've never been more confident, but he doesn't need me to say that to him. The attack is tomorrow, and I could lose him. I think the shock of realising that when I woke up this morning told me everything I needed to know about my feelings for him.

"Can I get Colton?" I ask him, knowing what I ask as we stand outside his bedroom door.

"You want us both? At the same time?" he asks me.

"I love you both," I whisper, not knowing what I would do if he said no right now. I look over my shoulder to see Colton coming up the stairs.

"I came to say good night. Everything okay?" he asks as he walks over to us. I look up at Nikoli, who merely nods and opens his bedroom door.

"Come in?" I ask Colton, whose eyes widen, but he steps closer, gently kissing me and leading us into the room. I break away from the kiss and walk back to the door as Colton looks around. Nikoli switches on a dim lamp on his desk as I shut the door behind me. The room is bigger than I expected it to be. There is a big dark wooden bed with white sheets, and a balcony that overlooks the forest. The floor is carpeted and there is a desk, two large wardrobes, and a full standing mirror in the room. There isn't much personal, but then I can't see too much with the dim light. I walk over to the balcony, looking at the moon in the sky which seems larger, and the sight of it almost full just reminds me of the attack tomorrow. I feel Nikoli move behind me, seconds before he moves my hair away from my neck and kisses me gently. His hands run down my arms, pulling my cardigan off. Colton steps in front of me, taking my lips in his and his hands slide down my chest, making my heart beat faster.

"We can stop now if you want," Nikoli whispers, and I turn around, running my hands up his chest as I shake my head. Colton starts kissing my neck, his hands still on my body.

"I don't want to stop. I want you, Nikoli. I love you and Colton. I want this, I want us," I say, and his slight intake of breath is the only sound in the room before he kisses me. Nikoli slides his hands down my sides, lifting me up. I wrap my legs around him as he carries me to the bed where he lays me down. Standing up, his eyes never leaving mine, he pulls his shirt over his head. Colton lies down next to me on the bed, watching as I pull my shirt off, and he follows suit. Nikoli finally crawls onto the bed, kissing me again; this time, pressing his whole body into mine. I gasp when he starts moving downward, kissing my neck, reaching my chest. He pulls my bra down and takes one of my nipples between his lips, sucking and gently nipping, as he uses his other hand to unhook my bra. Nikoli keeps moving down my body, kissing my stomach and undoing the button on my jeans. Slowly, he pulls them down, taking my lacy black underwear with it. When he kisses my core, it sends pleasure throughout my body, and I moan and wriggle on the bed as I slide my hands into his soft hair.

"So beautiful," Colton says and leans over me, kissing me hard. His hands start rubbing my hard nipples in the same motion Nikoli uses with his tongue against my clit. I gasp when Nikoli moves up my body; he had taken his jeans and boxers off, at some point.

"I like to watch. You first," Colton says, as he and Nikoli look at each other. Nikoli kisses me, his hands running over my breasts, making me want him even more. When he is lined up, he breaks away from our kiss and looks at me for permission.

"Yes. I want you as my mate, Nikoli," I tell him, and he moves a hand to my hip. He presses his lips to mine again and thrusts inside me at the same time. My back arches as pain racks through my body and I hold back a whimper. It soon passes, though, as my body heals itself, and I'm left with nothing but the pleasure of having him inside me. As he starts to move, his kisses become slower, more passionate. Every kiss is drawn out, his lips assaulting mine as he moves inside me, slowly building up my pleasure.

"God, Harper, you feel amazing," he says with a slight growl. I look up to see his eyes glowing as he looks down at me, I know his wolf must be over-riding his senses like mine is. I can feel her pushing against my mind, her happiness about finally being with one of her mates filling me.

"So do you," I gasp, as he picks up speed and moves his hand, running his finger over my nipple. The simple touch is all I need and I find myself letting go, shouting Nikoli's name. His thrusts become harder, faster, and I whimper a little when he bites down on my shoulder. The pain mixes with the pleasure and everything in that moment is perfect as he finishes.

I finally have one of my mates.

"Damn," Colton says, moving closer as Nikoli rolls off me and Colton replaces him. My body seems to take over as I flip Colton on the bed, happy to see he has taken all his clothes off. I kiss him as he grabs my hips and guides himself into me, making me moan out in pleasure again. I rock against him, picking up speed as I feel another orgasm coming, and two warm hands grab my breasts from behind. He flicks my nipples at the same time Colton speeds up and grabs my hips as he thrusts harder. I come instantly, tightening myself around Colton's cock, and he leans up, grabbing my neck with his hand and pulling me down to him. I don't expect him to bite me, but he does, his teeth piercing my neck. Instead of any pain, intense pleasure shoots through me at the same time I feel Colton finish inside me. I move my face closer to his neck, biting down until I taste blood, and the bond clicks into place.

And everything feels complete, for the first time in my life.

CHAPTER TWENTY-SEVEN
HARPER

"Harper, you need to wake up, my mate," Nikoli says, as I blink my eyes open to see him leaning over me. I smile, stretching a little and remembering the night before. I don't know what time we went to sleep because we couldn't get enough of each other. It was a night of learning about each other's bodies, about what we each like, and I don't ever want to change anything between any of us. The night was perfect. I look over to see Colton already out of bed, getting dressed, and he winks at me as he does his shirt up.

"I have to get everyone ready. They will be here

soon," Nikoli tells me, and reality crashes down on me. *It's today.*

"I can't lose you, not any of you. You're my family now," I say, and he smiles widely, moving closer and kissing me.

"We will fight them and win. But right now, we have to go and speak to everyone," Nikoli replies, sliding out of bed, completely naked, and it gives me a lovely view of his fantastic ass.

"Harper," he says, looking over his shoulder at me as he walks to his wardrobe. I smile at him and get out of the bed, pulling on my clothes from yesterday. I look in the mirror at my reflection and decide, other than the messy hair, I don't look any different. I feel different, almost older, and some part of me feels like I belong to Nikoli and Colton now. Like I'm complete, where it wasn't before.

"Harper, you okay?" Colton asks me.

"Yes, I just feel a little… I don't know how to explain it," I whisper but he hears me.

"We are connected now. I can feel extreme emotions from you and find where you are. You can do the same for Nikoli and me," he tells me, and I nod, walking over to him just as he pulls his jumper on over his shirt.

"Is there no way out of this?" I ask him, as he pulls me into a hug.

"No. We fight, and we win. That's the only way." He lifts my chin with his finger as he speaks, making sure I listen to every word. He kisses me hard and firm, a kiss I won't be able to forget, before letting go.

"We will make it out of this," Nikoli says as he opens the door to the bedroom. I let him lead us out of our bedroom and down the stairs. When we open the front door, dozens of wolves look back at us as they wait on the quiet driveway. I try to hide how nervous I feel in front of them all as Gold walks over, with a giant grey wolf at her side. I recognise the wolf as Erik and Gold looks nothing like I've seen her before. She has a leather outfit on, with daggers strapped to her thighs, and a crossbow in her hand. She winks at me when she gets close, and then Nikoli starts to talk.

"We fight today, and we fight for our pack. I once asked many of you to fight to get these lands back from the Hogs, and you did, and we lost some of our pack doing so. This time, we have allies." Nikoli waves a hand at Colton at my other side.

"We may not be wolves, and we may not know each other well, but believe me when I say, I will fight. My coven will fight to save the first place I feel at home," Colton shouts, and there are cheers following his words.

"We won then for a home, for the right to the land we were born on. I'm asking you to fight for something else today. I'm asking you to fight for our mates. For my mate, my alpha female," Nikoli says, and I step forward, sliding my hand into his.

"If someone told me a month ago that following a wolf into the woods would change my entire life, I would have laughed. But it did. Before I came here, I had only Colton. I didn't have a family, as I brought up in foster care, or any clue what that is or how it feels to have people you love. I hate to ask the family I have found, to fight, but here I am asking. I love Colton, my vampire and my mate. I love Nikoli, my mate and my alpha. *Your* alpha. Will you fight for us?" I ask, and the wolves bow their heads together before lifting them up to the sky, every single one of them howling. I smile up at Nikoli, who raises our joined hands and kisses my knuckles.

"They are coming soon, and I need to plan. You need to protect the women and children with Gold," he tells me, going over the plan we have spoken about. I want to be with him, but it's not smart when I don't know how to fight.

"Be safe," I say and press my lips against his. He kisses me back slowly before I step away and Colton pulls me into his arms, kissing my forehead.

"Keep each other safe, promise?" I ask him, and he nods, looking over my head at Nikoli.

"I will. As long as you are safe, I will fight to make sure you stay that way," he tells me and then kisses me. A kiss that shouldn't be public and Gold starts wolf whistling. I laugh and pull away from a smiling Colt.

"Let's go; they are coming," Gold says, moving closer to me, and Nikoli nods before walking through rows of wolves with Colton at his side. Seeing both my mates walking away is difficult; every part of me wants to run after them. I follow Gold through the front door, back into the house.

"He will be okay and so will we, but just in case, I want you to have this," Gold says, stopping outside the room and holding out a dagger for me. It has a black leather handle and a silver blade.

"Thanks, but I think I would be better off shifting," I tell her.

"You would, but I still want you to have this."

Gold doesn't wait for a reply as she opens the

training room doors, and the faces of many women and children in the pack look back at us. Snow walks over with Arisa at her side, a worried expression crossing her face, but she smiles when Arisa runs up to me, and I hug her. I look to see Light being held tightly in the arms of a vampire that I don't know, an older woman who came with all the vampires yesterday. I will have to remember to ask Colton who she is, but Light seems to trust her.

"Are the silly pigs going to go away soon?" Arisa asks me, and Snow answers before I can.

"Arisa, why don't you go and play with the other children over there?"

She nods, letting me put her down, and runs over to the ten or so children seated around a big pile of toys. The women are spread out on the floor throughout the room; some reading and some attempting to do anything other than look worried. I turn my head towards the window when I hear a loud growl, the sound echoing around the room.

"They will make it," Gold says, holding my hand. We spend the next two hours pacing the room, waiting for any news, but we don't get any. I hear growls and loud bangs, but feel nothing other than a slight bit of anger from Nikoli and worry from Colton. Suddenly, a woman screams out and holds her chest, bursting into tears as Snow runs over.

"Her mate died. They say you can feel it," Gold whispers to me. I stand up and walk away from her, going to stand by the doors and hope no one else will die. The woman's loud cries are something I will never forget.

"Someone is coming," Gold says as she walks over to me, stopping at my side by the door. I don't think as I pull the door open and step out into the corridor, expecting to see one of my pack.

"Little wolf...I've been looking for you," the Hog shifter from the car park says, stopping a few steps away from me, with his two friends at his side.

CHAPTER TWENTY-EIGHT
COLTON

I place my finger against my lips, telling my sister to be quiet in the tree opposite me. I look down, seeing the men in their human forms, and some of them have already shifted into hogs. Disgusting creatures they are, with their large circle-shaped bodies, black hair sprinkled around them, and large sharp teeth. You can just about see their beady eyes under the long hair around their faces. I do a quick count, finding there are twenty of them here, and I can hear more coming through. I would guess that they split up and came into the pack in groups, like waves of attacks. I bet they sent the weakest in first and then the strongest will follow.

"Oh, boys," Belle says, before jumping out the tree with extremely fast speed and landing her swords into the backs of the two hogs underneath her. The rest of my family jumps out of the trees, killing them in similar ways or running after the ones who try to run away.

"Attack!" I shout, jumping out of my tree and lifting my own two swords. The three hogs near me charge and I throw one of my swords straight into the head of one of the hogs and use my other sword to slash at the legs of the hog that gets to me first. He squeals and falls to the ground; unfortunately, his massive body slams into mine and knocks me into the tree. I push him off me, just in time to see the other hog running at me, its head down and those sharp teeth aimed at my stomach. I jump into the air at the last second and the hog slams its teeth into the tree, getting itself stuck.

"Colton!" I hear my sister scream, a scream filled with pain, and I scan the trees for her. My heart nearly stops when I see her being held down by a naked man, two boars at his side. One of her swords is lodged in her stomach. I see red when I run over, cutting off the head of the man holding her down, and the hogs turn to me. I pick a dagger out of my belt, holding it at my side as they both charge at me. Hogs are stupid and don't even think about me jumping in the air, then down on top of them. I slide both my sword and dagger into the heads of the hogs, pulling them out and running over to my sister. I pull the sword out, replacing it with my hand as I hold down on the wound. I need to get her out of here.

"Colton," I hear Nikoli behind me, and I turn to see him running over with Tam and Erik at his sides.

"Let me, I can heal her," Tam says, pushing me out the way after I nod and he places his hands on her stomach.

"We killed thirty of them," Nikoli tells me.

"There were twenty here." I look around at the bodies that my family have killed.

"She will be ok, but I need to get her back to the house and heal her further. Apparently, I can't heal vampires as well as wolves," Tam says gently.

"Ok. I will cover your back to the house. Thank you for saving my sister. I will owe you a debt," I tell Tam.

"You do not; you're pack to us now," Tam replies, as he lifts Belle in his arms.

"Run in front of me. I will sort anyone out that comes close to you," I tell Tam.

"*Go!*" Nikoli shouts, and I turn around to see at least twenty hogs running at us. Nikoli shifts, into a massive black wolf, and I turn around, pushing Tam's back and urging him towards the house. He runs fast and I pull two more daggers out my belt as I look around. Five hogs race out of the woods in front of us, just as we see the house, and surround us. Tam places Belle on the ground and we stand in front of her on either side.

"Here." I offer him one of my daggers.

"For the Forest pack," Tam says, nodding at me.

"For the Forest pack," I repeat his words, just as the hogs charge at us.

CHAPTER TWENTY-NINE
HARPER

"**H**ow did you get in here?" I ask, watching as the man smirks and steps forward, just as Gold comes out of the room and shuts the doors behind her. I can't believe these hogs got past my mates, the vampires, *and* all the wolves. *Something is wrong.*

"Oh good. I was getting bored," she says, seconds before she pulls a dagger out her belt and throws it at the hog who spoke. Unfortunately, seconds before it would have stabbed him in the heart, he catches it. I watch in shock as she jumps into the air, unclipping another dagger and landing on the back of one of the hogs. She quickly jams the dagger into his throat, before jumping back and knocking the legs out from under him with one kick. I watch in shock, not used to seeing her move like this; I didn't know how dangerous she was.

"Your friend seems busy," a voice says behind me, and big arms wrap around my chest.

"No!" I cry, remembering the dagger in my hand. I slam it into the man behind me and hear his deep gasp of pain seconds before his arms fall away. I run around him, towards the back doors. I make the mistake of looking back when I get to the door and see the man shift before my eyes, into a massive hog. It has two large teeth and a big round stomach covered in black fur. Its beady eyes glare at me and blood pours from one of his front legs where the dagger must have hit him. I pull the door open and shut it, before running into the woods. My wolf presses against my mind, begging me to take over. When I hear the door slammed open behind me, I stop running and do the only sensible thing I can think of. I shift myself and the moment my wolf takes over, she charges at the hog. The wolf knows it's weak and smells the blood he has lost, which only makes her angrier, wanting to kill him more. The hog slams into me, both of us falling to the forest floor. He stands up, charging over to me as my wolf shakes off the hit. I lean down and let out a loud growl, which vibrates around the forest and I know my wolf is calling for Nikoli; for our mate. I call in my mind for Colton too, shouting for him, even when I know he won't be able to hear me. Only seconds later, a louder, darker growl responds behind me, and then a large wolf presses against my side as he walks over. I don't take my eyes off the hog, but I would know Nikoli anywhere, in any form.

"*He hurt you. This is my kill, Harper,*" Nikoli says in my mind.

"*All yours,*" I reply, hearing Nikoli only growl back as a response.

I let my alpha finish the fight, watching as he jumps on the hog and kills him quickly. I mentally will myself to shift back, feeling the cold air of the forest and blinking my eyes open. I smile at Nikoli's wolf as I try to cover myself up a little and look back at the house. I nudge Nikoli forward and walk again, stepping over the broken back door. In the corridor, I see three dead hogs at Gold's feet, as she pulls a dagger out of one of them and wipes it on her thigh.

"Here." Snow comes out the room, shutting the door behind her, and offers me a male shirt. I pull it over my head, as she strokes Nikoli's fur and Gold comes over.

"Congratulations on winning the fight alpha, and our new alpha female," Gold says with a wink and Nikoli howls loudly. The sound of the pack howling back and the joy I can feel in the howls will be something I won't forget.

"Where is Colt?" I ask, starting to get panicked.

"He was bringing Tam and Belle back to the house; she was hurt," Nikoli says, and I run around Gold towards the front door. I can only hear the sound of my heart pounding as I pull the front door open. I just know Colton is this way; I can feel him.

"Colt!" I shout, when I see him walking out of the forest with Belle in his arms, Tam limping at his side. His eyes light up when he sees me, and I run straight to him. He is covered in blood, as is Tam, but they don't look hurt. I can't sense Colton in any pain.

"You okay?" I ask, breathless, and Tam pulls Belle into his arms.

"I need to get her inside, she has been out too long," he says.

"I can carry her," Colton offers.

"I'm healed, just sore. Don't worry," Tam tells him, and starts walking towards the house. Colton pulls me close to him, kissing me hard and resting his forehead against mine.

"We won, and we are safe," he says in a whisper.

"We did," I say.

CHAPTER THIRTY

HARPER

"You look incredible," Nikoli says, as he strolls into the room and looks down at me in my long, tight red dress. It's strange to wear a red dress when the night I got bitten, I wore red, and that night changed my whole life. I glance over at Nikoli, who is dressed in a full suit, his hair styled neatly to the side. He looks so handsome. We lost five wolves in the fight, but Nikoli said we were still lucky not to lose anymore. We had a funeral for them and grieved their loss, as did the mates they left behind.

"So do you. I was mad to let you out of bed this morning," I say, knowing that the last two months since the fight, all we have done is stay in bed. We have been spending every moment together, with Colton too.

"Wow, are you trying to give me a heart attack?" Colton says, walking out the bathroom, dressed in a suit, with his hair perfectly in place.

"Is that a compliment?" I chuckle when he kisses me and leans back.

"Definitely," he replies.

"We can go straight back to bed after the ball," Nikoli tells us. I mentally sigh, but keep a smile on my face for him as I walk over.

"I wish it was over already then," I say as I lean my head on his chest. The ball is an annual event for different shifter packs to meet up and make alliances. I'm interested in meeting all the other kinds of shifters tonight, and Nikoli is nervous because the royal family is coming too. We haven't told them about the vampires living here, or the mating. It isn't against the rules, but it's still going to be an awkward conversation. The ball hasn't been held at our pack for fifty years, and the pack has been running around trying to get everything perfect for tonight. Nikoli invited Colton and his entire coven to permanently live here after the fight. They are staying in the house for now, but they have taken some land just inside the pack lands, and started building their own house.

"I'm going to check on Belle before joining you in a bit," Colt says, sadness lacing his tone. Belle hasn't woken up from the fight and we don't know what's wrong with her. Tam has taken it personally that he can't heal her. He spends all day, every day, trying to figure out how to wake her up. Colt and his family aren't coping well with the fact Belle is ill. We all think there was something on the sword she was stabbed with; some kind of poison or magic.

"Okay, give her a kiss from me," I tell Colt, and he nods before walking out. I really hope she wakes up. Despite not knowing the vampire very well, she still fought for my pack.

"I hope she recovers soon. I don't want any more losses for the pack," Nikoli says, and it's his way of saying he is worried about Colt, not that he would admit it. I take his hand, letting him lead us out of his room. We walk down the stairs, which are even decorated, with roses around the bannisters. When we get to the bottom of the stairs, we take a left, straight into the ballroom, which is full of our pack and some other people. Nikoli told me earlier that we should stand by the door and greet people as they come in. I smile and wave at Gold as she walks in, dressed in a long gold dress that has a split all the way up to the top of her thigh.

"Looking hot, Harper," she says, causing me to chuckle.

"Thank you for inviting us," Nita says, walking in with Trevor and Light at her side. Light has a white dress on, with little crystals down the sides. She gives me a wave, with a cheeky small smile.

"It was never an invite. You are part of my pack, my family now. Your place is here," I tell them and Nikoli nods at me, in agreement. Nita gives me a broad smile, as does Trevor and Light, before they walk into the ball. We greet five couples – all wolves, I think – and then three men walk into the room. They nod at Nikoli and me, and I notice straight-away how they all look similar. They must be triplets or something. They are huge, with brown hair and expensive suits.

"Welcome. It's been a long time since we last spoke," Nikoli says, and holds a hand out to the man in the middle. He has a massive muscular body and a cheeky smile.

"Ah, I remember. We got drunk and had an interesting night. But I see those days are behind you now. You have a lovely mate," he says, and Nikoli laughs.

"Yes, this is Harper. Harper, these are the annoying triplets and the three alphas of the Bearlay pack." Suddenly, it clicks.

"So, you're bears?" I ask, and the one on the left laughs.

"Good guess," he tells me, looking around the room.

"We heard about your troubles. We could have helped if you'd called on us," the one on the left says, his tone serious.

"You know other packs aren't allowed to get involved with mate disputes," Nikoli answers.

"We should get out the way. The royal family was just behind us," the guy on the right says.

"We should catch up soon, but you have an alliance with us," the middle one says, and then they all walk into the room as Nikoli nods, stepping back and placing his hand on my back. Just inside the room, Gold walks past us, and all three bears watch her carefully, then look at each other. They quickly follow her over to a table, and she crosses her arms as they try to talk to her. It's amusing, but I wonder what they want with Gold. They seemed to know who she was straightaway, and she does not look impressed.

"Don't you both look amazing," Snow says,

walking in with Erik and Arisa next to her. Snow looks lovely in a tight white dress, while Erik is in a suit. Arisa is wearing a pretty pink dress and runs up to me.

"You look like Little Red Riding Hood," Arisa tells me, as I kneel down to hear her.

"We do have a lot in common." I wink at her, and she laughs.

"My mate," a deep, loud male voice says from the doorway. Arisa stops laughing, and I look up to see a man standing next to an old posh-looking couple. He was the one who spoke, and it's clear he is the prince, judging by the suit and crown he has on. The prince is staring at Snow, who steps close to Erik when he holds a hand out to her.

"I'm sorry, but you're mistaken," she says, and I let Arisa go as she runs over to her mum.

"No, I'm not," the prince says, looking between Erik and Snow. Erik growls slightly, and Snow shakes her head, looking away. It's only then that I notice how silent the room is.

"You are," Snow snaps back and picks Arisa up. I watch as she storms off into the crowd of people and towards the other doors in the room.

"She is your mate? The one you told me

about?" the prince asks Erik, who watches him closely and then looks over at Snow.

"Yes, mine," he says, and storms off after Snow and Arisa.

"What just happened?" I ask Nikoli quietly, just before the royal family walks over to us.

"Trouble, my little wolf," he replies.

Hello, and thank you for buying my book! You're amazing, and I can't tell you how much I appreciate your support. A review would be much appreciated, and I would love you for it, as every review helps me a little bit, and I love reading them all! This is Book One of the Forest Pack series, and the next one will be Gold's story. It's a reverse harem with some bears, and maybe a certain rogue wolf. The third book will be Snow's story. I also plan to write a story for Arisa and Light when they are grown up too.

A big thank you to Jen, Taylor, Anna, Meagan, Amanda and all my ARC readers, who make it possible for my books to be readable. They are all amazing. Come and say hello on my Facebook page, Twitter, or my website listed below. I post teasers, new covers, and giveaways in my Facebook group.

Bailey's Pack.

Thank you to all my family for their support as I wrote this book. Thank you to my husband for feeding me when I forgot to eat and my children for not destroying the house.

**<u>Please keep reading for Chapter One of
Run Little Bear (The Forest Pack Series #2)</u>**

<u>...</u>

LINKS

Here are all my links,

(I love to be stalked so if you have some free time...)-

Join my FB Group?-

https://www.facebook.com/groups/BaileysPack/

♥Like my FB Page?-

https://www.facebook.com/gbaileyauthor/

Be my FB friend?-

https://www.facebook.com/AuthorG.Bailey

Add me on Twitter?-

https:twitter.com/gbaileyauthor

🖤Check out my website?🖤-www.gbaileyauthor.com

🤍Follow me on Amazon?🤍-

http://amzn.to/2oV9PF5

🤍Sign up for my Newsletter?🤍-

https://landing.mailerlite.com/webforms/landing/a1f2

v0

The King Brothers Series-

Izzy's Beginning (Book one)

Sebastian's Chance (Book two)

Elliot's Secret (Book three)

Harley's Fall (Book Four)

Luke's Revenge (Coming soon)

Her Guardians Series-

Winter's Guardian (Book one)

Winter's Kiss (Book two)

Winter's Promise (Book three)

Winter's War (Book Four)

Her Fate Series-

(Her Guardians Series spinoff)

Adelaide's Fate (Coming soon)

Saved by Pirates Series-

Escape the sea (Book One)

Love the sea (Book Two)

Save the sea (Coming soon)

Only One Night series-

Strip for me (Book one)

Live for Me (Coming soon)

The Marked Series (Co-written with Cece Rose)-

Marked by Power (Book one)

Marked by Pain (Book two)

Snow and Seduction anthology-

Triple Kisses

The Forest Pack series-

Run Little Wolf- (Coming soon)

Protected by Dragons series-

Wings of Ice- (Coming Soon)

CHAPTER ONE OF RUN LITTLE BEAR (THE FOREST PACK BOOK TWO)

GOLD

"Why do I always have to play bait?" I ask Erik as he smirks at me and leans against the car. It's getting ridiculous that I'm always the one who has to pretend to be clueless and innocent as I walk up to the rogue. So sexist.

"Because you have that innocent look. If I walked in that bar now, they would know I'm here to kill them." Erik shrugs.

"It's because I'm a girl, isn't it?"

"Maybe," Erik teases.

"I'm just as good as you in a fight; maybe even better," I tell him, and he just grins at me.

"You keep telling yourself that, sis," he replies.

"Have you spoken to Snow yet?" I ask, and he glares at me.

"She won't speak to me about him, if that's what you're asking," Erik mutters, moving off the car and looking away from me.

"So, you're avoiding your best friend and your mate. Brilliant work, brother," I reply.

"Says you, who is avoiding three bears who claim to be your mates. You avoid your problem just as much as I do," he states.

I don't respond as I walk away from him and up the entrance of the bar. Those bears must be wrong, and they have been saying the same thing for the past year, since I met them at the ball. I've had nothing but roses, presents, and invites to their pack.

"Hey…pretty little thing," a man says, his face shadowed as he leans against the outside of the bar. I try to ignore the wave of disgust I feel looking at him and walk myself into the bar without replying. The bar is packed when I walk in; drunk humans everywhere, and it takes me only a minute to spot the rogue wolf I've been looking for. He's in human form, looking a state as he drinks a shot. His clothes have seen better days, and I can't help running my eyes over him and his very strong-looking body. The wolf turns to glance at me when I walk closer, his dark green eyes locking with mine, and his scent hits me. He smells amazing, and I don't know what to do as we both stare at each other.

"Do you even know why you're hunting me, darling?" the wolf asks. His voice is deep and husky as he puts his finger up and another shot is placed in front of him. I don't recognise his accent, it's definitely foreign.

"The Royals send the order, I don't usually check the details," I respond, sliding into the seat next to him, but never taking my eyes off him.

"Just a paid lackey, huh? Not checking who you're hunting because you trust the Royals so much?" he says, and then laughs.

"Just come outside with me. I will take you in, and I don't have to kill you," I say, watching as he takes another shot.

"I recognise you, Gold," he states, assessing me.

"You don't look or act like a normal rogue. If you had heard of me, you would run out the door," I say, used to rogues doing that.

"That's why the back door is already locked, and your twin is waiting outside the only open door," he tells me, knowing our plan already.

"You're going to make this difficult, aren't you?" I tilt my head to the side as I look at him.

"No one bit, as I won't hurt you," he replies, confusing me further. "Don't you know who I am to you?" He chuckles, and I slide off my chair, shaking my head as more of his scent hits me. It makes me want to fall to my knees, and I'm trying hard not to move closer to him, like my body wants me to.

"You can't be…" I say.

"You're my mate. I can smell it, and I know some part of you recognises that," he chuckles. I shake my head and turn my back on him as I walk out the door. I can't hurt him or be anywhere near him; they need to send someone else to do this. Erik frowns at me when he sees me walking out, and then he looks behind me. I turn to look at my rogue following me out of the bar, stumbling a little as he walks. The wolf is drunk.

"Don't kill him, you can't." I hold a hand up to Erik, who frowns.

"It's our job, Gold. What the hell are you doing?" he asks me.

"Protecting my drunk mate, it seems," I say, and turn around in time to see my rogue fall face flat on the floor with a thud.

\-

Please keep reading for an excerpt from Marked by Power (The Marked Series, co-written with Cece Rose)

PROLOGUE OF MARKED
BY POWER

T he dim lighting in the room does nothing to hide the predatory look on his face as he stalks around me, moving in a circle. I keep trying to move with him, to keep my eyes on him and my back away, but he's just too quick. He shoots flames to my left, and I jump to my right, narrowly avoiding the hit. I try to counter with air, calling on my mark. I aim low, hoping to strike him off balance. He blocks my attack with a simple swipe of his hand.

A cool jet of water flows from his right hand; he doesn't aim it at me, but at the floor. I stare at him in confusion, when suddenly, the water begins to cool and freeze over. I struggle not to slide across it. I lift my left hand and command fire, using fire's heat to melt the ice, and the steam creates a wall between us. I try to use it as a screen to attack, but he simply uses his air ability to clear his vision again.

I back up a few steps to keep out of reach, but he pounces, crossing the space between us. Within seconds, I'm pinned down onto the blue mat by his weight. I struggle to get loose, completely forgetting to use my magic in order to assist me.

"Miss Crowe," he whispers in my ear softly, his deep voice sending shivers right through me.

"Kenzie," I mumble.

"What?" he asks.

"Please call me Kenzie," I whisper.

"Miss Kenzie Crowe," he utters softly, his cool breath against my neck making me shiver.

"Yes?" I whisper, looking up and catching the heated look in his green eyes.

"You would be dead six times over if I was really trying."

Today is the first day of the rest of my life; my initiation into the marked academy. I glance around at all the other seventeen-year-olds dressed in traditional white, as we walk across the rocks. Most look excited, a few nervous, and one even looks a little bored, but I'm calm. I'll be happy whether I get one power, eleven, or any of the numbers in between. I feel a hand slip into mine, and as I look around to see Kelly, I smile at her.

"Aren't you nervous?" Kelly asks.

"Nope. It doesn't matter what happens. I've just got to last three years in this school, and then I'm back to the plan. It's hard to be nervous when you're not invested," I answer softly, aware of the quiet around us, and not wanting my voice to echo in the darkness of night.

"I am," she whispers. "What if I only get one? My dads will be so disappointed. Mum will be happy with whatever, but those two, they just have so many expectations," she adds.

I frown. I know her dads have always been pushing Kelly to be a high achiever, but seeing her worry like this makes me glad that my own fathers only want me to be happy. The three of them have always shown me support in whatever I want to do, and my mum is the same.

"It'll be fine, Kells, I promise," I reply, squeezing her hand tightly.

She shoots me a grateful smile, and then her eyes widen as we reach the cave entrance. The entrance is considerably large for a cave and is mostly filled with water, but for a narrow, uneven ledge that runs along one side.

One by one, we file onto the ledge in alphabetical order, walking slowly and carefully across it. Kelly lets go of my hand reluctantly and slips in behind me, walking so close I can feel her breath on my neck. I'm glad her surname follows mine: Crowe and Curwood; I'd hate to think of her doing this part without me.

We follow along the trail until I see the people in front of me seemingly vanish into the wall. I drag my fingers along, waiting for the crack I know is meant to be there. The guy directly in front of me steps to the side and vanishes. I follow his steps and feel my fingers leave the wall, finding the gap. I slip through after him and walk in darkness for a moment until I see where the narrow gap opens up.

Torches line the walls, the flames flickering and casting shadows everywhere. I carry on, following behind the guy in front, and I hear Kelly closely behind. The path opens into a large cavernous space. A serene pool of water lies between us and a grand, golden, double door. The doors are covered in the twelve markings of the marked, six on each.

There are three people cloaked in black standing in front of the door. One stands to the side by a gong, holding a long striker. Another stands slightly to the other side, gesturing for us all to file into the room. And one stands in front, a long gold chain hanging around their neck; the master of today's ceremony.

We all file into rows in front of the water. Once side by side again, I feel Kelly's hand slip back into mine. We kneel as instructed and wait for the rest to file in. Once we are all waiting, kneeling patiently, the master of the ceremony steps forward.

"Welcome, new students, to The Marked Academy. One by one, your names will be called, and you shall enter the water. The water here is all the way from Ariziadia, and will activate your dormant powers. You are to submerge to receive your marks at the sound of the gong. Once blessed by the water, you shall declare how many markings you received, before passing through the doors. However, if you are not blessed by the water, you must leave immediately. Do you all understand?"

A mixture of affirmative answers and head nods roll across the room as we indicate our understanding. I feel Kelly's hand squeeze mine tighter, the worry of not being blessed clearly getting to her.

"We shall begin," the ceremony master says.

I can feel the tension in the room as everyone stares forward, waiting for the blessings to begin.

"Jacob Addison," the robed figure to the left calls, their deep voice carrying across the otherwise silent room. The guy kneeling on the front row furthest to the left stands and makes his way to the pool of water. His hunched shoulders are the only sign of his concern as he slowly wades through the water till he reaches the centre and stops, nervously looking around. I count my blessings that I'm not first. The pressure of going before everyone else must be overwhelming.

The robed figure to the right bangs the striker against the gong, and Jacob submerges himself in the water, going completely under. We all watch and wait with bated breath for him to rise. After what feels like forever, he emerges, spluttering as his hands pat against several parts of his body. He must be counting his marks.

"How many markings?" the deep voice calls.

"Seven," Jacob replies. He looks around and catches the looks of who I assume to be friends, giving them a thumbs up, before wading the rest of the way across the water. He walks up and past the robed figures before slowly pushing the grand-looking door open and stepping through, the door closing softly behind him.

"Joshua Allen," the robed figure calls, wasting no time in continuing.

The next guy stands and makes his way into the water. The gong sounds, he submerges, and then emcrges again.

"How many markings?" the robed man asks.

"Four," Joshua answers, his voice wavering over the simple word.

Without looking back, he crosses through the water and walks up past the robed figures, and leaves through the golden door as the guy before him did.

"How many more people before us?" Kelly whispers to me softly.

"Twenty-two," I whisper back. "Just be glad our surnames don't begin with Z."

I shoot a smile at her, which she returns nervously. 247 of us needing to be blessed; I'm glad I'm not the robed guys right now. Turning my head, I cast my eyes across to the guy sitting at the back at the far right. Nope. It's him I am glad not to be, his knees will be aching like hell by the time he gets called.

I turn my attention back to the ceremony, watching each person stand as they are called, and step into the water. They all receive marks; the lowest three and the highest ten earning ten. The one with ten gets some impressed looks from other students, who are kneeling and waiting. As I watch Liam Cartwright walk through the large doors on the other side of the water, I take a deep breath.

"Mackenzie Crowe."

Despite expecting it, I freeze when my name is

called. I wasn't feeling nervous before, but the water suddenly looks so much more daunting. With so many still in here watching, I feel the pressure mount. What if I only get one? It doesn't matter so much to me if I don't have powers, but others may think less of me for it, and I have to put up with these people for the next three years. What if I stand in the water and have nothing, nada. If I'm not marked, what would happen then? It's not as if that is common, but it's been known to happen; I wouldn't be the first. Not marked, not human, but unmarked.

The unmarked are born of a marked line, but not deemed worthy of power. The ultimate failure in the eyes of my people. I gulp as I stand, straightening my shoulders as I walk the short distance to the water. The water is completely still, not a ripple in sight. I dip my toe in first, feeling the cold shoot straight into me, chilling me to my bones. I cast a glance back at Kelly. She shoots me an encouraging smile and mouths something at me, but I can't make out what.

I turn back, looking straight at the door ahead, and step into the water. I wade in until about waist deep, in the centre of the pool. I look up above, the gap in the ceiling of the cave letting the moonlight in. The glow of the full moon is strangely comforting.

The gong sounds, and I submerge a second after, letting the icy-cold water cover me, closing my eyes as my head goes under. I feel the chill of the water make me shiver, and I start to wonder how I will know if I have been blessed or not, when I feel a burn on my left ankle. That's one. Another on my right hip. That's two. Fuck, my ribs! I clutch my ribs with my hands as a burn starts there as well. And then suddenly, pain strikes across my body in several places all at once. The water now feels hot, not cold. I pull myself upright, so I'm standing, shaking slightly. I look down at myself and try to make a count of all the marks, using pain as an indicator of the ones below clothing. Both ankles, both thighs, both hipbones, my ribs, two on my back, both wrists, and I feel a burn on the back of my neck. Wait, how many is that? I do a mental count. Twelve. That's got to be wrong. I count again.

A throat clears, drawing my attention to the hooded figures, knowing I need to announce my markings. I try to count again, coming up with the same answer; twelve. How is that possible?

"Miss Crowe?"

"Tw-twelve," I stutter quietly.

"I'm sorry?"

"Twelve," I repeat more clearly. "I have twelve marks."

Whispers start around the room. It doesn't take long for the volume to rise, and for it to become shouting. Twelve marks, it's impossible. I can hear people yelling things like "liar," "deceit," and "check her" as I swallow and slowly make my way across the rest of the pool.

I stand before the robed elders, waiting for them to allow me to pass and enter The Academy. One of the figures steps toward me and holds out their hands, palm up, requesting my own. I place my hands in theirs and they turn my hands over and inspect the two markings on my wrists. The symbol of flames on one, and water on the other. They release them and twirl their fingers, asking me to turn around. I do as they say, facing the other students who are waiting for their own initiation to begin. I feel fingers lightly brush my thick, dark hair out of the way and then trace over the marking on my neck. I shiver from the gentleness of the touch.

"I don't need to see anymore," the man's voice says quietly. "This is the twelfth marking on your neck. I've never seen anyone wear this mark. I believe what you say is true."

I release a breath I didn't realise I'd been holding. At least, he isn't going to make me strip in front of most of my classmates on the first day. Now, that would have been embarrassing.

"Continue into the school, Miss Crowe. We will speak with you once the ceremony is over." He says it softly, so the words don't carry.

I nod my head and slip past him, eager to get away from all the eyes watching me. I reach the large door and push; it opens far more easily than I'd expected. I walk through and allow the door to close behind me, cutting off the stares. Just as the door is about to close, I hear them call Kelly's name.